THE JULES VERNE PROPHECY

THE JULES VERNE PROPHECY

LARRY SCHWARZ
&
IVA-MARIE PALMER

ILLUSTRATIONS BY EUAN COOK

Christy Ottaviano Books
LITTLE, BROWN AND COMPANY
New York Boston

Copyright © 2023 by Larry Schwarz and Iva-Marie Palmer
Illustrations copyright © 2023 by Euan Cook

Cover art copyright © 2023 by Euan Cook. Cover design by Tracy Shaw.
Cover copyright © 2023 by Hachette Book Group, Inc.
Interior design by Michelle Gengaro-Kokmen.

Christy Ottaviano Books
Hachette Book Group
1290 Avenue of the Americas, New York, NY 10104
Visit us at LBYR.com

First Edition: June 2023

Christy Ottaviano Books is an imprint of Little, Brown and Company. The Christy Ottaviano Books name and logo are trademarks of Hachette Book Group, Inc.

Library of Congress Cataloging-in-Publication Data
Names: Schwarz, Larry, author. | Palmer, Iva-Marie, author. | Cook, Euan, illustrator.
Title: The Jules Verne prophecy / Larry Schwarz and Iva-Marie Palmer; illustrations by Euan Cook.
Description: First edition. | New York : Little, Brown and Company, 2023. | Series: Jules Verne prophecy | "Christy Ottaviano Books." | Audience: Ages 10–14. | Summary: "When a mysterious book by the beloved writer Jules Verne falls into the hands of three unlikely friends, they begin a treasure hunt adventure through Paris"— Provided by publisher.
Identifiers: LCCN 2022038308 | ISBN 9780316349819 (hardcover) | ISBN 9780316350198 (ebook)
Subjects: CYAC: Books—Fiction. | Verne, Jules, 1828–1905—Fiction. | Summer schools—Fiction. | Schools—Fiction. | Paris (France)—Fiction. | France—Fiction. | LCGFT: Action and adventure fiction. | Novels.
Classification: LCC PZ7.1.S33658 Ju 2023 | DDC [Fic]—dc23
LC record available at https://lccn.loc.gov/2022038308

ISBNs: 978-0-316-34981-9 (hardcover), 978-0-316-35019-8 (ebook)

Printed in the United States of America

LSC-C

Printing 1, 2023

To Mom
—LS

To my sons, Clark and Nathan.
Raising you has been the best adventure
your dad and I ever embarked on. Thank
you for taking my heart on journeys
I never imagined possible.
—IMP

All that is impossible remains
to be accomplished.

—Jules Verne

CONTENTS

ATTENTION!
ALL STUDENTS MUST READ!

In this seminar, you will be learning about Jules Gabriel Verne, French novelist, poet, and playwright. Born in 1828, Verne's most prolific years were between 1863 and 1905, when he published fifty-four novels in the Voyages Extraordinaires (Extraordinary Journeys) collection. Of these works, the most well-known are *Journey to the Center of the Earth*, *From the Earth to the Moon*, *Twenty Thousand Leagues Under the Sea*, and *Around the World in Eighty Days*.

To this day, he remains the most translated author of science fiction in the world and has been named the father of science fiction. With his adventure stories, he hoped to elevate the form, and with his legacy, he has.

But Verne is to be appreciated as more than a literary figure. In his works, then science "fiction," he predicted realities, meaning he wrote of scientific discoveries that would not be invented until later: everything from air-conditioning and the moon landing to fax machines and sky writing.

Was he a visionary or simply an extremely imaginative writer? We'll discuss these questions and many more over the course of our time together.

—Professor M. Bessier

CHAPTER ONE

Why Save the Chase Scene for the End?

Thursday, June 18, 10:22 a.m.

BOOM! I SEND AT LEAST ONE HUNDRED TINY EIFFEL Tower key chains to the ground and almost bobble off my board as I roll over a few of them. The mustached guy selling tourist stuff runs alongside me and yells, "Idiot! As-tu perdu la tête?" I think he asked if I've lost my brain but my French isn't great. Maybe he said, "You break it, you buy it." I push off hard to get away from him before he tries to charge me. I definitely do not have the euros for all those busted towers.

I also don't have a copy of *Twenty Thousand Leagues Under the Sea*, a book by Jules Verne marked up with my notes. Notes I can use for the test I have to take in a little over an hour. Oh, I'm also short approximately thirty-six Starbursts (half red, my favorite, which I'd been saving to eat last).

And WHY don't I have those? Because some punk kid just stole them from me!

And I can see him, a bit ahead of me...

My board makes a clackity-clack noise on the bridge's wooden slats and I slide in front of a guy in a suit who's holding out a ring to a lady in a dress. As I clip his shoulder, he drops the ring so it's headed right for the water. I lean off my board, catch the ring in my hand, and pass it back to him in one motion, and how did I just do that and no one got it on camera?

"Pardonnez-moi! Pardonnez-moi!" I excuse myself, as I photobomb several clumps of tourists taking selfies with the Eiffel Tower in the background.

I can't slow down. I need my backpack. And I need to count all those Starbursts and make sure that kid didn't eat any.

I spot the twerp. He has curly blond hair and is about ten years old—his red T-shirt hits his knees and his pants are baggy, but not in a cool way. His hat is beat-up and old-timey, like he's in a school play and his character has

to sell stuff on the street. He takes a second to look back for me. We're off the bridge and on the Quai Branly and somehow there are even more pedestrians here, and more traffic, and he slips across the street just as the waiting cars and scooters get the green. French people drive smaller cars than we do in the States but they make up for the size difference by going faster than anyone does in Connecticut. And they honk like crazy. I have to jump back up on the curb as a Vespa almost cuts me in half.

The backpack thief must feel good about himself because he's stopped on the other side of the street, looking right at me. With a grin, he unwraps one of my Starbursts—of course it's a red one—and pops it in his mouth.

It's like he knows the reds are my favorite.

I wish I had something to throw at him, but all I have on me is my skateboard and there's no way I'm giving this joker anything else of mine.

As I kick off into the street, a Peugeot driver leans on his horn and screeches to a stop in front of me. I jump from my board and it rolls under his front tires as he yells something at me—I don't speak great French yet, but I know it's not good. I hop on the hood of his car and back down—landing right on my board. Then he flips me off. I definitely know what that means. But, how could he be mad? That was awesome!

The kid must realize that he shouldn't have stopped to eat my candy because when he sees me coming, he spins away, sprinting toward a street of little shops.

I'm gaining on him.

Just one more good kick and I'll be able to grab him by the back of his T-shirt. I stretch out my arm. Then I hit a wall of oatmeal. No, I do not hit a wall made of gooey thick breakfast cereal. More like, it feels like my lungs have been dipped in the stuff.

I'm having an asthma attack.

I sit down on the curb next to a guy doing caricature drawings of tourists. They're honestly pretty good, as long as you're a girl and you have long curly hair and a teeny nose or you're a guy and you have long curly hair and a teeny nose.

I reach into the pocket of my jeans and pull out my inhaler. I take a deep inward breath and…oxygen. The oatmeal dissolves. I'm able to stop the asthma attack.

I peer down the street and see the little jerk watching me. Maybe he saw me have the attack and feels bad? I spring up from the curb, grab my board, and run right at the kid. He sees me and turns a corner.

I'm there in seconds but there's no sign of him.

I've officially been robbed by a ten-year-old.

CHAPTER TWO

How I Wound Up Here

"OWEN, WHAT HAPPENED?"

I stared angrily at the mostly empty alley—a cat slunk out from between two trash cans but no sign of the kid and my backpack. I keep telling my new friend Nas Shirvani he can use French with me, but he asked in perfect English.

I turned around to see that Nas was not alone. Rose was with him. Rose Bordage, the last person I wanted to witness a little punk getting away with my stuff.

I wiped my eyes. They were watering a bit from my asthma attack. I wasn't crying.

"He's got my book," I said. I didn't mention the Starbursts.

"C'est très dommage," Rose muttered. She was right. It was très dommage—super bad. My marked-up copy of *Twenty Thousand Leagues Under the Sea* was gone. And not only would it have been helpful for the test we had coming up, but our instructor, Professor Bessier, also told us that if we didn't have the book, he wouldn't let us take the test.

Wait, I guess I should explain who these people are. I sort of got caught up in the chase through Paris and maybe you're a little lost. (But you have to admit, even if the twerp got away, that chase was bonkers. I had to lead with it.)

That's not where all of this starts. Nope. I'm new here in France. And I wouldn't have been chasing my stolen Starbursts through the streets if I'd stayed in New Haven, Connecticut.

I wanted to do nothing for summer break, except skateboard with my friends. Okay, and play video games, hopefully perfect my cannonball in Darren Leach's pool. Paris was not on my radar.

Then my mom came home one night and said that she'd been selected as a guest lecturer at the Institut Lagrange de Paris. She's the youngest ever physics department head at Yale so she gets invitations all over the country, but usually it's a day at Berkeley in California or a trip to New York to give a TED Talk. Sometimes, she'd take me with her, but other times, she'd leave me some pizza money and ask our neighbor Mrs. Fagerstadt to check on me. This time, she'd been invited to Paris for the summer, and guess whose life she thought would be enriched by the experience?

I told my mom that maybe I'd be fine eating pizza for an entire summer. Mrs. Fagerstadt liked me, and my mom and I could FaceTime. But she said that was too long for us to be an ocean apart, so my plan was a no-go.

And instead of Mrs. Fagerstadt and pizza, my mom had signed me up for a séminaire, which is French for "seminar," which is English for SUMMER SCHOOL. THE WORST. She knew someone who knew someone who helped her reach out to an instructor for an exclusive course that was usually offered to only French kids from ritzy schools, like Rose, and a select few French scholarship students, like Nas. I'd been taking French since I started middle school, so Mom thought being immersed in the language would be good for me.

"You'll need something to do while we're there," she'd said. Then, when she gave me a packet about the class she signed me up for, she added, "And this might take care of that unfortunate Reading and Composition grade."

Oh, that.

Most of my grades at Charles Goodyear Middle School were pretty good, even without a ton of effort. I'm not bragging. I guess, the same way I've always had asthma, I've also always been pretty good at school stuff. Maybe it's how the universe evened things out for me. But my Reading and Composition grade could have been better. Like, a lot better. There's more to it than that but we don't need to go there.

Darren Leach and some of my other friends were jealous I was going to Paris. So I tried to get interested and read the packet about what I'd be learning. But Jules Verne...? *Twenty Thousand Leagues Under the Sea*...? Nope.

Nothing against Jules Verne, who I'm sure was a big deal in his time, but science fiction written a hundred years ago seems pretty backward. Back then, a car with giant buggy wheels was a sensation. What could an old dead guy possibly have to say about technology that would be better than the actual technology I used every day?

I grimaced. "Can't we just watch the movies?" I said. It was half joke and half serious.

Mom handed me my backpack and told me to get

packed. "We'll see a movie and eat pizza in France."

The first few days weren't so bad. Mom had some time to settle in and that meant we spent a whole Sunday at flea markets finding new things for the apartment we'd rented. Mom loves old stuff and she'd gotten me a new (well, old) camouflage backpack because she wanted me to upgrade for my new French life. Then we'd gone to a French McDonald's, which they call McDo, and where the fries might actually be even better than in the United States.

But then she started work and I started the seminar. And now I was chasing a kid who'd stolen my flea-market backpack so I could feel like the biggest loser ever while my new friend Nas and the coolest girl I'd ever met gave me sympathetic stares.

"Professor Bessier is not going to like this," Nas said.

"It's still better than your first day of class, non?" Rose asked. I cringed.

She was right. This was better, but I didn't want to think about that first day again.

CHAPTER THREE

Séminaire Day One

Monday, June 1 – Two and a half weeks earlier

MY FIRST DAY OF THE SEMINAR WAS TWO DAYS AFTER WE'D arrived in Paris and one day after my mom dragged me to all those flea markets. (Our house is filled with dusty, breakable artifacts. My mom's job is to think about the future, so old stuff makes her feel comfortable.)

I shouldn't say *dragged*, because after I finally got out of bed (jet lag!) and was walking around cluttered stalls with my mom for a half hour, it was kind of fun. I was going through some old concert T-shirts with French words on them while my mom dug through these crates. She pulled something from the bottom of one and said, "I think you should have this." It was the camouflage backpack, with sort of tarnished hardware and a lot of pockets. "It has more personality than your JanSport."

"I don't really need it," I said, even though I liked it.

"Maybe not but I can tell you *want* it," Mom had said. And then she'd had a conversation with the stall-keeper in way better French than mine and voilà! I had a new backpack.

On the walk back, she carried the backpack because she'd used it to hold a vintage French teapot she'd found, and she showed me the route from the apartment we were renting to the collège, which is French for "school." But between the McDo still digesting in my stomach and my jet lag coming back in a big way, I think I missed some of the street names my mom pointed out.

So on Monday, the day the seminar started, I got a little lost. My plan had been to be one of the first kids there, so I could choose who looked like someone worth hanging out with, but the courtyard was already packed with people.

The school was holding several seminars, for a bunch of different ages. A lot of the kids were way taller than me.

It was hotter than I'd expected and my shirt was sticking to me, but I kicked up my board and toted it through the crowd.

The French kids looked more like they were about to take pictures for a fashion magazine than go take notes. No one had on baggy shorts or hoodies or track pants and T-shirts like in Connecticut. I stood next to a pillar and scouted for someone who looked like they were alone, too. On the other end of the courtyard, there was just one other kid who wasn't with a group. He was also about the same height as me. He had on a hoodie like all my friends back in New Haven, wore big earphones, and was moving along to music. As he bobbed his head, he looked up, saw me, and nodded— like a "Hey, what's up?" nod toward me, or at least I hoped so.

Bingo. A cool kid at last.

I decided to go over to him and say hello. Or "bonjour," like you say in French.

I was thinking about how to make my *bonjour* sound great as I walked toward him, making my way through various groups. Most of them barely noticed me, though I got a dirty look from an older girl when my backpack bumped her shoulder. The center of the courtyard was tighter and I stepped right on someone's foot. It was a woman selling coffee from a cart and she glared at me. So I pretended I wanted a coffee by saying, "Un…coffee?" The barista rolled her eyes and said, "Un café américain, non?" And I nodded, figuring I wasn't going to push my luck and try to get something with whipped cream. I ordered whatever a "café américain" was.

When she handed me the steaming cup, I hoisted it in the air like I was toasting the headphone kid, and he gave me a strange look as I slugged some back. I was really expecting the French coffee to be like the stuff I sometimes got at Dunkin' Donuts—like a supersweet milkshake with caffeine. But this was thick like lava. And definitely not sweet.

My face crinkled up as the hot, bitter coffee made its way down my throat. My eyes started to water. Then some kid with an actual cigarette blew a huge cloud of smoke right at me.

I tried to turn away but a gust of the smoke hit my eyes and nostrils and I started to cough. I spit coffee into the air and the crowd parted. It seemed like everyone was watching as my projectile coffee arched in the air and landed…

Right on a blond girl's head. She touched her face, then glared at me. She was so horrified, I might as well have picked up a dead bird out of the garbage and started eating it. She stomped up to me in her combat boots and

16

said something in French I didn't totally get. But from her tone, it sounded like it probably meant, "Are you kidding me, you gross weirdo?"

The best thing to do, I thought, was to make a joke. It works more often than you'd think. Problem was, my French was only Connecticut good. So, I grinned at her and flipped up my skateboard. But I hit it a little too hard, and instead of flipping up into my hand, it flew up right toward the girl's face. She caught it—it was a pretty good move—and shoved it back at me. Across the courtyard, I saw the headphone kid laughing hysterically.

Then the girl smiled a little. So I said, in the best French I could, "Veux-tu un café?" (or "Do you want a coffee?") It was pretty funny, I thought. But she held up her bottle of fizzy water, which I thought meant "No, I've got a drink," until she opened the cap and sprayed it at me. Then she stomped off and left me with a wet shirt.

Of course, after that, we started talking and became BEST friends immediately. Have been ever since.

That was not what happened.

Even though the water was cold, I yelled "Ow!" extra loud and flailed my arms. Everyone nearby scattered. Total disaster.

Mercifully, a lady in a pink suit came out and called for students in the Jules Verne seminar. She led us to a classroom and instructed us to sit and wait for our professor.

But *of course* that girl was in my seminar. Rose Bordage. I sat as far away from her as possible.

Then the instructor came in and wrote his name in neat letters across the board: *Professor Bessier*.

He was tall, thin, and pale in a way that would glow in the dark, and he was hunched over an open book he held in his palms. His thick-rimmed glasses slid down his nose, and he pushed them back up the bridge as if he were irritated they weren't cooperating. He began to read, speaking slowly, in a deep voice that I wasn't expecting.

"'The monster emerged some fathoms from the water, and then threw out that very intense but mysterious light mentioned in the report of several captains. This magnificent irradiation must have been produced by an agent of great shining power. The luminous part traced on the sea an immense oval, much elongated, the center of which condensed a burning heat, whose overpowering brilliancy died out by successive gradations.'"

He slammed the book shut and stared at all of us, like we had already disappointed him. Then, in a much quieter voice, he said, "But of course it wasn't a monster. It was a submarine. And not just any submarine but the *Nautilus*. A seafaring vessel far superior to any we've witnessed in fiction or reality, if you ask my opinion. And Jules Verne's greatest invention. You may ask other Verne scholars and they may give you a different answer, but they would be wrong. Jules Verne's *Nautilus* is unmatched for its design, its capabilities, its brilliance…and it all sprang from Verne's own mind. While he wrote many works that are wonders, for this part of the seminar, you will be learning everything there is to know about *Twenty Thousand Leagues Under the Sea*." He stared at me and didn't smile.

He was so into the speech, I thought he would have given it even if we weren't there. But okay, at least a high-tech submarine was cooler to read about than the other inventions he supposedly predicted, like fax machines.

As Bessier started calling roll, I realized I was sitting next to the earphones kid.

He stretched a hand out to introduce himself. "Moi, c'est Nas," he said. "Nas Shirvani."

With relief that someone in class would talk to me, I put on my best accent and introduced myself. "Je m'appelle Owen Godfrey."

"Tu es américain," he said.

I tried to think of something to say in French that I could pronounce well. I needed a friend. And I needed that immersion to click soon.

Behind me, someone cleared their throat. I glanced back to see Professor Bessier looming with an annoyed look on his face. I hadn't even seen him move, and I checked the front of the class in case there was a second Professor Bessier still standing there. Nope. He was just quick and really creepy.

Then Bessier swept back up the row to continue calling out our names.

Nas and I traded a look that said, *That's one scary guy.*

"Just so you know," Nas whispered in perfect English. Good accent and everything. "You're a terrible coffee drinker, but you get points for style."

CHAPTER FOUR

Turns Out, Paris Is Pretty Cool

NAS IS FROM THE TWENTIETH ARRONDISEMENT OF PARIS, where he lives with his mom, dad, and a younger brother and two little sisters. He's smart. He'd gotten into the seminar on a scholarship, and his parents had been thrilled. Nas was thrilled, too, because the seminar gave him an alibi. While his parents figured he was studying, he'd be able to DJ and skateboard. His parents didn't like him skateboarding because he'd broken his arm doing it when he was eight, and they didn't think he should DJ until he was older.

When he said he liked to skateboard, I felt like I'd done a good job spotting the cool kid in séminaire. Nas even knew where the coolest skate park in the entire country was.

After class that first day, Nas invited me to go with him to Le Dôme.

"Is that a museum?" I asked in French.

"Non, bro," Nas said. "It's for skaters." He nodded at my board.

I was suspicious. After a few days in Paris, I didn't feel like it was a skate park kind of place. The parks I'd seen seemed more like the parks in movies, with trees and gardens for people to have important conversations while enjoying a picnic.

But I was wrong.

Le Dôme is amazing.

It wasn't always a skate park. Le Dôme is the back courtyard of the Palais de Tokyo art museum. There's a bunch of stairs—perfect for skate tricks—and a wall made of sculpture. It's a lot of ancient people—guys fighting monsters and half-naked ladies in togas carrying jugs of water—but it makes skating at Le Dôme feel like you're trespassing at a famous museum. Plus, if you shoot a video of yourself nailing a sweet jump off one of the stairwells leading down in front of the frieze, it's an instant classic. In the center of the courtyard is this shallow fountain that's sort of like a pool you'd never swim in. The water is greenish and algae films on the surface.

Learning about Le Dôme was like being in on a secret everyone knows about. Even non-skaters hang out there.

So, skating there had become our routine since we started the seminar.

It's also where we were earlier today when my backpack got stolen. Class was starting late so we could study, but it was an open-book test. In other words, a whole Thursday morning for Le Dôme! I was working on my ollies while Nas set up his laptop and speakers.

And guess who was there? Rose. Cringe. She was sitting next to the pool with her combat-booted feet straight out in front of her.

Since the day we first met, Rose and I still hadn't spoken. The idea of being friends with her seemed impossible. The thing I noticed about Rose was she was smarter than most of us. When she answered a question—often in rapid French I had trouble understanding until I thought about it a bit—Bessier would clap his hands together like he was thanking some higher being for having one gifted student. Then he'd have her say the answer again in English. Which I knew was for my benefit.

I lightly elbowed Nas. "Rose is over there," I said. "I'm going to ask her to study with us." Not that we were studying, but we *could* have been.

Nas's eyes bugged out.

"T'es sérieux? T'as failli vomir sur elle," Nas said. I knew that meant, "Really? After you basically puked on her?"

"Histoire ancienne," I said. Immersion was working!

"Well, she's, like, from one of the richest families in Paris." Nas shook his head as if this fact made Rose a lost cause.

"Oh, good. I thought she wouldn't want to talk to me because I doused her in my caffeinated backwash." I stared at him. "So why would her being rich mean she wouldn't want to hang out with us?"

"They're the most powerful collectors of basically everything," Nas said. "I heard that if her dad wants some bones from halfway around the world, he can have them next-day air."

"That's her dad," I said. "Maybe she wants some friends with their skin still attached."

Nas gave me an "I tried" look and put on his headphones as he opened his track list. "If you want to talk to her, go ahead," he said. "I bet she's a snob."

Nas calling Rose a snob seemed unfair, but in the short time I'd known him, Nas had told me that rich, important people avoided his arrondissement. I thought if I could get Rose to hang with us, it might help change his mind.

Rose was obviously smart, but if she were stuck-up, why would she be at Le Dôme, instead of some fancy breakfast spot? I got up and went to talk to her just as Henri, this other DJ, came by to hang with Nas.

In a fake deep voice, I said, "'I am not what you'd call a civilized man!'"

It's a line from *Twenty Thousand Leagues Under the Sea*. Captain Nemo says it.

Rose looked at me like I was definitely not civilized but also not funny. Maybe she hadn't gotten to that part of the book yet. Or maybe I was terrible at being cool in Paris with Rose Bordage.

At that exact moment, and it had to be intentional, Nas played the sound of a record scratch, and a funeral march cut through the air. Harsh.

I was about to explain my reference to Rose— because why wouldn't I make an awkward situation worse by talking about it some more—when I saw a kid with a cool camouflage backpack walking past this bench with a statue of a guy and two horses with sea serpent bodies underneath it, like they were holding it up.

The backpack was a lot like mine. I nodded to myself in approval. I had to admit, people in Paris really did have good taste.

But then I looked back toward Nas on the steps, the steps where I'd left my backpack, and saw that mine wasn't there. The kid had my backpack!!

I jumped on my skateboard—why had I carried my skateboard over to Rose but not my backpack?—and took off after the thief. I sped through the traffic in front of the park, my face wobbling as I clacked on the Debilly bridge over the Seine.

And I already told you about that. (But video would have been way better.)

CHAPTER FIVE

After the Chase

Thursday, June 18, 10:30 a.m.

WITH THE KID LONG GONE AND NAS AND ROSE IN FRONT of me, I was reminded of the reason we were standing there in the alley by Quai Branly.

"That kid took my backpack," I managed, my breathing returning to normal.

Nas had his headphones around his neck, his backpack dangling from one shoulder, and his laptop under one arm. "We saw."

Rose came toward me with a bottle of water. For a second, I thought she might spray me again. But then she handed me the water and asked, "Are you okay?" Like a nice person, not a snob. I shot Nas a look that said, *See? She's nice!*

I took a sip and she said, "You're not going to spit on me again, are you?"

"Buy me a coffee and we'll see," I said. We were laughing at this, and I thought it almost might be worth it that my backpack had been stolen, even if my Starbursts and book were inside. But…my book! "Our test! It's in…"

Rose peered at her phone. "Il est dix heures et demie," she said. "We have…"

"…Less than one hour until our test!" I sputtered. The test that I'd get kicked out of and auto-flunk for not having a book. "What am I going to do?!"

"We could tell him you're sick," Nas said.

"I don't think Professor Bessier would believe you," I said. "He doesn't even trust us to go to the bathroom." The guy had some strict classroom rules.

"I could help you study," Rose said.

"But we need the book or we can't take the test!" I kicked the ground. "You guys go. Don't miss the test for me."

We were sitting on the curb. Together. I was surprised they didn't ditch me immediately. And kind of glad. Nas looked up and down the alley, like he thought my book would just drop from the sky. Then he turned around, doing a double take at something behind him. He tapped me on the shoulder. "This is weird," he said. "But it looks like the answer is right here."

He was pointing to a store right behind where we were sitting. The windows were so cobwebbed and grimy, I couldn't tell what was on display. "What is that? A dust store?"

"The sign," Nas continued. It said LIBRAIRIE CLEM-ENCEAU in faded letters. In France, *librairie* is what they call a bookstore; libraries like we have back home are called *bibliothèques*.

"That is weird," I said. "It's like that little jerk led me right to this store. Maybe they sell Starbursts, too."

Rose was already opening the shop's heavy black door. "Not that weird, you two," she said in French. "Paris has hundreds of bookstores."

If the shop looked dusty from the outside, it was just a way to advertise there was more dust on the inside. The sunlight that filtered weakly through the front window illuminated the bonus puffs of dust that seemed to rise as we walked past the stacks of books that covered every surface except a narrow strip of floor. To walk in some places, you had to turn sideways to fit through the paths formed by stacks of books that rose in front of shelves. *Also* filled with books. There was no way this place wasn't a massive fire hazard.

How would we find a copy of *Twenty Thousand Leagues Under the Sea* in the mess?

Sidestepping my way toward the front of the store, where I'd seen a man behind a cash register as we'd walked in, I sent a pile of books toppling. I fumbled to get them back into place but the pile had been balanced between two similar sloping stacks. It wasn't something I could replicate. I was starting to sweat, and my heart was thudding loudly. Please, not another asthma attack. I left the books on the floor.

Nas and Rose were still scanning the shelves and piles and my stomach lurched. It was bad enough that I didn't have a book for the test, but if we didn't get out of here soon, my friends would be late for the exam because they were helping me.

I cleared my throat, forcing the bored clerk to look up. "Pardon...où sont les livres de Jules Verne?" I asked, hoping he'd understand I wanted to find the Jules Verne books.

The clerk, whose black heavy-metal T-shirt had a picture of a skull with snakes curling out of its eye sockets, shook his head. "Jules Verne?" He made one of those "not sure" gestures and it was obvious he wasn't going to help me look, so I went back to collect Nas and Rose.

"Forget it, guys," I said. "We're not going to find anything here. I'll have to deal with Bessier's wrath."

"Are you sure, Owen?" Nas said.

"Maybe if you tell him yours was stolen," Rose suggested.

Ha. Like I hadn't tried that kind of excuse a million times in New Haven. I'd made up so many pets hungry for my missing homework that I could open a fake zoo. (I didn't think Monsieur Bessier would care even if he believed my absolutely true excuse.)

My shoulders slumped, even without my backpack weighing me down. I sure could have used a red Starburst. "I'll figure something out."

As I squeezed back through the stacks, something hit me. Like, really hit me. A big book came out of nowhere and knocked me on the head. "Ouch!" I said, bending down to pick it up. It was massive and definitely old. I was about to balance it on top of the nearest pile when I saw the name on the spine.

Jules Verne.

It was called *La Prophétie de Jules Verne*.

A Jules Verne book had landed in my lap. Okay, landed on my skull.

It wasn't the book I needed but it was big. I figured it was one of those books of his collected works. And *Twenty Thousand Leagues Under the Sea* was so famous, it *had* to be in there. I didn't want to waste time opening it to check because the test was in about twenty minutes.

"I'm getting this," I said, hefting the book from the floor and showing it to Rose and Nas.

"It's pretty," Rose said, extending a hand to touch the embossed cover. She pointed to a corner that was damaged, like it had been dripped on. "I wonder if there was a leak in the roof up there." She glanced toward the top of the shelf.

"It's better than nothing." I grinned, suddenly feeling a little better. Even without my notes, I could still do okay on the test.

I set the book next to the register and the heavy-metal guy looked at it like I'd put one of those creepy hairless cats on the counter. It was like he'd never seen a book before. He would not be winning Employee of the Month. "Hmm," he said. "Not sure what this costs. Um, how about…?"

He flipped it over, and I bit my lip, praying he wouldn't ask for too much. Then my stomach dropped. I had no money at all on me. My euros were in my backpack.

"Ten euro?"

"Uh." I reached in my pocket and pulled out a two-euro coin and a fifty-cent one. But then Rose opened her purse. She thrust a bill at me, a ten-euro note.

"Only civilized men have wallets, Captain Nerdo," she said.

33

"Merci," I said, as relief washed over me. Not only would I have a book but my uncivilized man line hadn't been a total bust.

The clerk handed me the book like he was anxious for us to get out of there so he could go back to not helping anyone.

"After this day," I said as I held the door for Rose and Nas to follow me out of the store, "I hope the rest of my trip here isn't as boring."

I didn't have to worry about that.

CHAPTER SIX

Me + Test = UGH

Thursday, June 18, 11:15 a.m.

BACK OUTSIDE, ON THE BANKS OF THE SEINE, WE STOOD there talking about how crazy it was that of all the books to fall on my head, it had been a Jules Verne book. But I had this weird feeling I was forgetting something. "I feel like we're supposed to be someplace," I said.

Suddenly, Rose made a gulping noise and charged away. "That test! Bessier's test! Our test!"

Nas and I both spewed out exclamations that would have gotten us in trouble if adults were to hear them. But in French. Another point for immersion.

"It was so cool finding the book, I forgot about the test," Nas said. "Give me the book. I'll put it in my bag." He was already jogging to catch up to Rose, so I tossed it to him. Without slowing down, he stuffed it in his messenger bag. I tucked my board under my arm and sprinted next to them.

Despite the rushed, panicked, sweaty feeling, it was kind of nice. Nas, Rose, and I had been through a battle—a mini one—and now we were bonded for life or something. I hoped so, in a way.

We arrived at the collège just as the last few students were trickling back from lunch. We ran through the courtyard and into the building, then raced down the hall and filed in past Professor Bessier right before he shut the door.

We slid into our seats. Rose turned around and said, "Good luck" to Nas and me.

"Here goes nothing," I muttered to Nas. Everyone began to take out their books—thin little paperbacks of *Twenty Thousand Leagues Under the Sea.*

Nas smirked as he pulled my book from his bag and handed it to me. "You'll be fine," he said. "It's open book, and your book is enormous."

I hoisted the massive thing onto my desk with a giant thump. A cloud of dust spurted forward from between the pages. Nas and a few people near me started to cough.

Bessier was coming down our row with the test papers. He dispensed them facedown and quickly, like he didn't want to get too close to any of us. As he got closer to me, the back of my throat tickled. I was still breathing okay after my last hit of the inhaler so I knew I was only nervous, not having an attack.

I inhaled through my nose as Bessier dropped a test on my desk. The tickle in my throat seemed to race upward and I had to cover my face as I sneezed a huge, wet sneeze. I chanced a look at Bessier, who looked thoroughly grossed out. At least he didn't say anything about my million-pound book.

"You may flip your tests over and begin," he said, taking a seat at his desk. Bessier then pulled out a set of paints and a tiny paintbrush that he was using on a small figure of a man in a big underwater helmet, like the crew members in the *Nautilus*. The guy really lived and breathed Jules Verne. It was bizarre.

Nas patted my shoulder. "Don't look so scared," he said. "It's not life or death."

No, but it was life or finding out what Bessier did to students who flunked tests.

I turned over my test paper, still wishing I had my

book with all the passages I'd marked up. I squeezed my eyes shut, hoping I could get a mental picture of some of the words I'd underlined.

The questions were all essays. I read a few.

> The *Nautilus* submarine is commanded by Captain Nemo, whose surname translates to "No one" in Latin. The mysterious captain chooses this name for himself. Why does he do so?
>
> Even though submarines didn't exist during Jules Verne's life, he thought up the *Nautilus* submarine for *Twenty Thousand Leagues Under the Sea*. He writes that it is a long cylindrical vessel. Now describe, citing the text, the layout of this incredible invention.

Whew. Okay, these weren't easy, but I had a giant Jules Verne book, and I told myself I could do this. I flipped open the book to a page near the beginning, hoping to find a table of contents. I closed my eyes and waited for the dust to settle. Then I peered down at the page in front of me.

You know that saying "never judge a book by its cover"? Well, never do that, because even though you'd think a giant book with Jules Verne's name on the cover would be full of everything Jules Verne ever did, my book was not that.

The page I was on had strange drawings that didn't look like any alphabet I knew. I flipped through the crusty pages as fast as I could, scanning for a title I recognized. But nothing. I saw pages with numbers or weird scribbles, and a few with handwritten notes in French. None of the pages with writing went on long enough to even be a Jules Verne short story, let alone a whole book.

I would not be able to cite the text of *Twenty Thousand Leagues Under the Sea* because I for sure didn't have the text.

My heart started to pound and sweat trickled down my back and armpits. I tried to stay calm as I flipped through the pages again, hoping the name *Captain Nemo* would materialize. But all I saw were more gibberish letters or strange pictures.

If there was anything more fun than an asthma attack, it was a panic attack, and I was having one.

And now, of course, was when Monsieur Bessier looked up from his figure painting and right at me. He smoothly unfolded himself from the chair and was standing over me after two steps.

"Are you having some trouble?" He was bent low, his pale face right up in mine.

I closed my eyes and inhaled a slow breath, holding it a few seconds and letting it out as gradually as possible. My heart stopped racing. I coughed with my lips pressed tight together and shook my head. "No trouble," I croaked.

Bessier kept standing there, watching as I folded my hands so I could stay calm. His nostrils flared like he was getting really tired of having me in class. Finally, he asked, "Where is your book, Monsieur Godfrey?"

Okay, I could reason with him. He'd give me a new book to use, right? "This kid... Well, I was studying and I left my backpack..."

Bessier raised his hand in the universal teacher gesture for "That will be enough excuses." Then he said, "I suppose *le chat a mangé mes devoirs*. Well, I've heard it before."

"Maybe I can..." I thought I could ask to come back later, or borrow a book, even though Bessier didn't seem like my biggest fan at the moment. But before I could say anything, his eyes cut to the book I did have.

"What is this?" He put a long finger down not on my book but right next to it. He was staring at the weird characters like they were giving off toxic rays that were penetrating his eyeballs and turning him a paler shade than he already was. Great, not only had I been robbed by a ten-year-old but I was also about to give my teacher a heart attack. But why?

"Mon Dieu," he said quietly, and not even to me. He was staring at the wall. "Where did you get this?"

By now everyone was peeking our way. Rose caught my eye and seemed like she was about to say something. I gave a little shake of my head. She shouldn't be in trouble for my problems. "Like I said, I got robbed and…" I was about to mention the store, the book falling on my head, the rush to buy it.

Bessier closed my book, using just the tip of one finger. "No, this will not do. Wait in the hall until the test is done."

I reached out to take my book back, and Bessier flattened his whole palm on top of the cover. "No, this stays."

I knew if I tried to argue, Bessier would never listen. I stood up, picked up my board, and shuffled down the row of desks. Rose and Nas both shot me looks that seemed to say, *You're dead.*

As if I didn't already know that.

CHAPTER SEVEN

What's French for Major Screwup?

WHEN I'D ONLY HAD AN HOUR TO FINISH THE TEST, IT hadn't seemed like enough time, but the wait in the hallway for Bessier seemed to take forever. I had nothing to do but sit on the floor and roll my board under my feet. I could see the courtyard, where a few students lingered and the woman who'd sold me my café américain cleaned up her stand before classes let out. My stomach growled to remind me I hadn't eaten. I missed my backpack full of Starbursts more than ever.

With five minutes left, I could actually hear people's pencils working faster. Then the bell rang. I took a deep breath and slumped down even further against the wall, waiting to be stared at by my seminar classmates. I'd been robbed by a small ten-year-old in weird clothes and banished to the hallway by a Jules Verne–obsessed teacher. Suddenly, this whole summer in France thing wasn't going great.

The door clicked open, and the hall filled with the sound of kids chattering, probably excited to be done with the test. If I hadn't been so careless with my stuff, I'd have been one of them. I could have invited Nas and Rose to go get a burger, or whatever French kids ate after brain-breaking tests.

I was picturing the plate of fries we'd share when I realized Bessier was standing over me. He had everyone's tests under one arm, and my book cradled against his chest, like it was a baby he was protecting from an avalanche. I scrambled to my feet.

"Professor," I began in French. "I can explain."

Bessier's head twitched left and then right as he peered down the hallway. "Not here," he hissed. "In my office.'"

I wanted to wait for Rose and Nas, though. But Bessier started down the hallway and turned when he realized I hadn't moved. *"Tout de suite!"* he said, meaning *"Now!"* I grabbed my board and trudged and trudged behind him. I'd have to text Nas later and see if he and Rose did okay.

Bessier's office was at the farthest corner of the collège, down a hallway that got narrower and darker the farther you walked down it. He stopped at a door, fished a key from his pocket, and slid it into the lock.

When he opened the door, I had to stop myself from saying, "I knew it!"

Just like I thought, this guy was way too into Jules Verne, and his office was Exhibits A through Z and back again. Every wall was covered with bookshelves lined with volumes that had Jules Verne's name on the spine. In the spaces without shelves was framed artwork—a retro-looking poster with a rocket that said *Journey to Mars* across the top, a painting of a massive octopus about to wrap a tentacle around a guy in a deep-sea suit, and a cross-section of the earth with a red-orange center. And stuff—old stuff, like compasses and goggles, a model of a hot-air balloon, and at least five or six different models of the *Nautilus* submarine. The office was packed, but neat. Nothing was dusty. Bessier's collection was really important to him, judging by how neatly it was arranged and the way he scanned the small office as if checking everything was still in its place.

Still, it was extreme. I wondered if Bessier slept in a bed-sized replica of the *Nautilus*, his version of the race car bed I'd had when I was six.

At the same time, it was interesting to see all that

Jules Verne stuff together like that. There was a style to it I could respect. He'd come up with all these ideas way before there'd ever been Marvel movies or *Star Wars*. If Professor Bessier hadn't been so Bessier-y, I might have asked him about some of his collection.

Bessier set the tests down in an ornate wire basket at the corner of his desk, which was clear of any clutter, besides the basket and a coffee cup shaped like a diver's helmet. The blackboard on the wall had recently been erased and washed. On the railing that held the chalk was a new-looking sponge held inside a squid-shaped dish.

I stood in the doorway, not sure if I should sit down. Bessier didn't say anything. Still clutching my book, he slipped off his leather loafers and put each foot into pointy green velvet slippers. Then he walked past me and clicked the door closed. He twisted the lock and turned toward me.

My fingertips tightened on the top of my skateboard. This was getting a little weird.

But I still sat down when Bessier finally pointed to a chair on the opposite side of his desk. He sat on the other side and put the book between us but with his bony hand on top of it, like he didn't want me to touch it. "Tell me exactly how you got this book."

It was showtime. I went through the whole day. Le Dôme, the kid stealing my backpack, the chase, and finding the bookstore. I told him how the book had fallen on my head, maybe hoping he'd think I'd been concussed and would let me retake the exam.

I didn't feel like he felt sorry for me, though. His eyes narrowed every so often, and a few times he cocked his head like he was trying to decide if I was a liar or not. But he wrote some of what I said down, and I thought that was good.

"And that's what happened," I said finally. "I'm sorry I didn't look out for my other book better." I hated apologizing, especially when it really wasn't my fault, but I hoped Bessier would like it.

He didn't. His normally pale face filled with color, and his cheeks flushed a dark pink. He cleared his throat. Then, in English, he said, "We let you in this seminar even though you had no familiarity with Jules Verne because your mother applied and gave evidence that you are a serious student." I wondered what he meant by "evidence" but didn't dare ask. Now he stood up, still with the book, like it had become attached to his arm. "We made special concessions for you. I speak my slowest French. I say things in English, for you! But this is too much! A boy steals your things and disappears, a book falls on your head. Do you think you are Jules Verne, making up stories? I am going to have to fail you."

46

He was standing with his back to the door, still looking at me. Without turning around, he unlocked it, letting it swing into the hallway.

"Leave."

I didn't even think to ask him to return the book.
The words *fail you* kept replaying in my ears.

What would I tell my mom?

CHAPTER EIGHT

Not My Finest Hour

Thursday, June 18, 2:23 p.m.

I COULDN'T EVEN SKATE HOME. THE WHOLE DAY SORT OF
fell on me all at once, like the book had, and I felt heavy
and slow and awful as I made my way home from the collège. My mind kept coming up blank as I tried to imagine
explaining to my mom how badly things had gone.

I wandered around the city, trying to decide how to
explain this to her. I was so nervous, I kept walking into
people. I almost stepped on some lady's little dog.

"Watch it!"

"Pay attention!"

No one in France liked me very much, but did people in *any* country like you if you were a massive screwup?

Maybe they could smell failure on me.

Trudging past some kids in a café sharing the plate of fries I'd have liked to share with Nas and Rose, I thought of how I got into this mess in the first place. In a way, it was my mom's fault.

The whole thing started with a *Great Expectations* paper. I'd read the entire book and thought the main character Pip was kind of unappreciative toward all the friends who helped him. So at first, I was writing a paper in my usual way, winging it, making jokes about how *Great Expectations* wasn't great, and honestly not putting in a lot of effort. But then Pip's whole attitude kept bugging me and I started a new paper, about the themes of friendship and loyalty in *Great Expectations*. I worked for hours finding examples and using a thesaurus and everything. When I'd finally finished, I was so proud, I emailed it to my mom. Then I remembered how my mom hates reading on the computer, so I printed her a copy and left it on the table with a note for her to read it when she got home from the lab. My mom works a lot—she has to—but she always makes time for me and always reads my papers.

The next morning, Mrs. Fagerstadt called to wake me for school, which she would do on mornings Mom had to leave extra early for the lab. When I went downstairs to make myself breakfast, my paper and the note hadn't moved. And I knew Mom had been there because she'd left her Einstein mug on the table. So she'd sat right next to my paper and hadn't even touched it!

Instead of remembering all the times my mom *had* read my essays and how, the week before, she'd left the lab early to take me to a skate park and then for pizza, I got really mad about my paper sitting there with no note from her or sign she'd touched it at all. That week, she'd been at the lab a lot and I was sick of being alone. So, because I figured she didn't care, I tore my good paper to shreds. Then I'd printed out the half-finished, no-effort paper and turned that in instead. I still don't know exactly why I did it, except for being really angry.

But the failing grade had made everything worse and that was how I ended up in this stupid Jules Verne seminar. That I was also going to fail.

I stumbled against a curb and crashed into a man walking a dog. A big dog this time. "Gamin," he said. At least the dog looked like it felt sorry for me, a pesky street urchin.

If I were my mom, I wouldn't want to spend time with me. All I did was mess up, on both sides of the ocean. How would I tell my mom that I'd failed, again?

I avoided going home for as long as I could. But after wandering for hours, my mouth was dry and my feet were sore, so I made my way down the narrow street. The sun was still out, but it felt much later and I was hungry. I hadn't eaten all day.

Maybe if Mom was here, we could eat together before I told her everything.

I hoped my last meal could at least be something good.

CHAPTER NINE

Make a Plan

I PUT MY KEY IN THE LOCK AND STEPPED INTO OUR APART-
ment. I was so relieved to be home that I temporarily
forgot everything awful that had happened. I chucked
my skateboard in the hall closet because it drove Mom
nuts when I left it out. I was about to take off my backpack when I remembered I didn't have it.

Then my stomach growled, like it wanted to remind
me I deserved to eat before I lost my appetite.

"Mom?"

My mom wasn't a loud person, but the total silence
of the apartment wasn't making me hopeful she was

home. I stepped down the narrow hallway and called out again, "Mom?"

My stomach growled and sank at the same time when I saw the pizza box and the note on the small table next to the kitchen. Big surprise, she wasn't home. At least I wouldn't have to tell her about getting kicked out of the seminar. But what if I'd actually had *good* news? I couldn't have shared that, either.

If I was going to spend the night feeling sorry for myself, I figured I should at least do it with a full stomach. I picked up the note. My mom had drawn one of her cartoons, a pizza wearing a beret, and out of its mouth was a word bubble that said, "I'm sorry to have missed you, O, but I had to pop in and leave again before going to an evening lecture. I hope you had a good day! I tried a new pizza and hope it reminds you a little bit of home!"

"It's just like home. You're not here," I said to the empty apartment. I was definitely being dramatic. My mom was doing her best at juggling me and her research. Two nights ago, she'd been waiting for me to get back and taken me to a teeny bowling alley on the Champs-Élysées so I could tell her how things were going. But, after everything that had happened today, I wished she was around now. And because she wasn't, I was mad.

I flipped open the lid and saw a pizza. But not a normal pizza. Not even a Hawaiian pizza. It was a snail pizza. Snails in their shells, on a pizza.

Did *Twenty Thousand Leagues Under the Sea* want to torment me by showing up on my pizza?

I had trouble believing that even French people liked snails on pizza. Poor Mom...I knew she meant well. This was like when we'd had to cancel a trip to Disney World and she'd gotten me two pet mice to make up for it.

I flicked a snail off my slice, half afraid it would slink away. But it just lay there. At least it was a dead snail pizza.

Captain Nemo would have eaten the whole pie. Probably even the shells. I didn't think you were supposed to like him. That first question on the test, about why his name translated to "no one," was because Nemo is a super-private guy, especially after his family is murdered, and thinks most of society is stupid. He goes off to an island and builds an awesome submarine just to keep his privacy. And he doesn't even explain himself. He says stuff like, "I have broken with society for reasons which I alone have the right to appreciate. So I do not obey its rules, and I ask you never to invoke them in my presence again!"

I kind of got it. I mean, real life could be a pain. Why not escape to the bottom of the ocean and make up your own rules? Then you wouldn't have to deal with grades or being expelled or your mom having to work nights when you wished she was around.

I knew that in the book, Nemo builds his sub because his family was killed, but maybe he was lonely before that. Maybe Nemo's mom had had a demanding job, too. That would explain how he became someone so used to being alone he built a super-insane submarine. I would invent a space-travel-ready skateboard if I could, and when things got to be stressful, launch myself for a little solar-system ride.

In the novel, the United States government thinks the *Nautilus* is a destructive sea monster, because something huge and green is sinking their ships, so they put together an expedition to kill it. And Nemo takes those characters prisoner. Like Professor Aronnax, a member of the expedition and the book's narrator, this kind of know-it-all guy. He's pretty impressed with the *Nautilus* at first, and how he'll be able to see more marine life than he ever thought possible. But Ned Land, the harpooner who's supposed to kill the sea monster, doesn't care about exploring the sea if it means being Nemo's prisoner. At the end, he finally gets Aronnax and this other guy to go along with him and escape the *Nautilus*, in the middle of this crazy storm. Now that I was thinking about it, maybe I liked

Twenty Thousand Leagues Under the Sea more than I realized.

At least, I remembered a ton of it.

Who needed an underlined copy of the book when I had my clearly awesome brain? Captain Nemo, I knew, would agree.

I wiped the snails off a slice of pizza, folded it, and shoved it in my mouth in one huge bite. Not terrible, if I didn't think about the snail slime that might be on the cheese.

Then I grabbed my board from the closet and raced down the stairs and out onto the street. The sun was still out because it went down so late here, something I hadn't gotten used to. I kicked off toward le collège, expertly weaving around pedestrians before they could yell at me for being an annoying, rude American.

I was an annoying, rude American who was going to get his professor to let him take his test.

CHAPTER TEN

A Visit with Professor Bessier

Thursday, June 18, 8:22 p.m.

PROFESSOR BESSIER'S SHADES WERE UP AND I COULD SEE he was still in his office when I rolled into the courtyard. It wasn't surprising that he hadn't left the school. He was definitely the kind of teacher I could only picture in the classroom or the office, surrounded by his Jules Verne stuff. I wondered if he even went out to eat or if he called a special hotline to order snail pizza to his desk.

I leaned behind a pillar and watched him scurry around the office. He was still holding the book. My book. Had he not even put it down? I knew he'd thought

I was lying, but it was a little nuts to be checking my book for proof.

Inching closer, I tried to decide if I should tap on the window or throw pebbles at it to get Bessier's attention. Bessier stopped his pacing, raced to his blackboard, and with the book still open in one hand, started to copy something from it. In class, he wrote everything in perfect block letters, but right now he wrote in a scribble. I squinted to read the words.

Then I realized they weren't words. Whatever he was transcribing looked like strange squiggles and lines, at least from where I was standing. This was getting weirder by the second. Maybe it would be easier to accept that I was kicked out of the seminar.

But no, it wouldn't. For one, I really liked hanging out with Nas, and now that Rose was in the mix, things were even better. And for two, my mom wasn't the type of person who got angry, but she definitely got disappointed, and that's a thousand times worse. I *had* to get Bessier to give me the test.

I edged closer to the window. I'd just tap on the glass, lightly, to get his attention.

My hand was in the air, about to knock, when Bessier fished his phone from his pocket and answered it. I couldn't hear what he was saying, but he grabbed the old book tighter and his face scrunched up angrily as he spoke rapidly into the phone. He must have been having an argument. Finally, he hung up, and I was so curious about what was going on, I forgot to knock.

I watched as Bessier walked over to one of the larger *Nautilus* models. It looked heavy, like it was made of brass that had been weathered, as if it had actually been underwater. The front end was curved into a spiral shape, painted silver and green, with a dome-shaped window at the top. The middle was oblong with a row of smaller windows running across it, and the spiral design at the front gave way to a texture like fish scales painted on the metal that eventually fanned out to a fin-shaped back end with another window along the bottom. He stood in front of it and bent his knees with a slight bounce, like he was about to take a foul shot in basketball. Then he pushed the *Nautilus* model until it flipped over. He

had a secret compartment built into his shelf! For a weird guy, he was also a little cool.

He put my book into the compartment and sealed it up. He seemed twitchy, looking behind him and even at the ceiling of his office, like he was being watched, and not just by me. It hit me like a ton of bricks: That dusty old book was a big deal. Bessier hadn't taken it from me because it was the wrong book. It was an important book.

But *what* about that dusty old book was such a big deal?

With one more glimpse over his shoulder, Bessier scanned one of his shelves and pulled down a different book, thick and old like it could pass for the one of mine he'd just hidden. He tucked it into a messenger bag. Then he kicked off the weird slippers from earlier that day and put on his shoes, a fedora, a scarf, and a black trench coat. It was summer, but maybe Bessier was so committed to loving Jules Verne that he even dressed like he was in one of his stories.

Whatever reason Bessier had for hiding the weird *Prophétie* book away, I could tell he really wanted it. And, in a flash, I realized I could tell him he could keep it only if he let me take the test. Genius idea.

I'd have to catch up with him when he left the school. I grabbed my board so I could find Bessier as he exited. But as I turned the corner, I saw him fling the heavy doors open and dash out into the courtyard. I was about to call out to him when a black car pulled up at the curb and two guys got out. They were wearing dark coats and hats, too. Maybe Bessier was in some kind of intense book club with a serious dress code.

Bessier had stopped walking when he saw the guys, but he didn't look afraid or anything. More annoyed, or angry. Like they'd brought the wrong books, too.

One of the guys pointed at the car and Bessier shook his head, but the second guy said something else, and Bessier muttered to himself and got in with them.

I watched as they drove away. I would have to convince Bessier to let me take the test tomorrow. Captain Nemo couldn't have come up with a better plan.

CHAPTER ELEVEN

The Day After the Test That Wasn't

Friday, June 19, 8:00 a.m.

I MADE IT BACK TO THE APARTMENT AND FELL ASLEEP before my mom got home, and when I woke up the next day, she was already gone. She had left a note at least: *O—Just need a few more days to get into the swing of things and then I promise we'll spend some more time exploring the city together. Maybe we can see one of those* Fast & Furious *movies you like (with English subtitles). Have a good day at class!* Then she'd drawn an octopus driving a souped-up submarine.

She'd left a chocolate croissant for me, too. A big step up from snail pizza. The whole setup made me feel better. I loved the notes my mom left me.

Out the window, the day was beautiful, prettier than the paintings tourists bought from artists on the Seine. The street was already busy with people starting their days, and the summery weather seemed to make everyone look more colorful than usual.

I was actually excited to get to class, see my friends, and make my little deal with Professor Bessier. I skated through the crowd and smiled at people, who smiled back. Okay, maybe Paris wasn't going so badly for me after all. And neither was becoming a Jules Verne expert. What would Bessier's face look like when I told him that I got it? Captain Nemo, Ned Land, and the *Nautilus* had made an impression on me, and I could take my test without my book. I wouldn't even bring up the *Prophétie* book he'd confiscated. He could keep it, as long as I could dazzle him with my knowledge of Jules Verne. I had Captain Nemo levels of confidence that this would work.

When I walked in, both Nas and Rose were already there. Rose jumped from her chair and gave me a hug that made me feel like I was returning from an epic battle. It was extra surprising but not horrible. When she finally let go, Nas said, "Everyone thought you got kicked out."

"I did," I told him.

"So, why are you here?" Nas said. "Bessier doesn't seem to like surprises."

I shook my head. "He'll like it if I surprise him by knowing the answers to our test without my book, and if I convince him that I think Jules Verne is half as cool as he thinks he is."

Rose nodded, agreeing with me. "Owen has a point," she said. "It's the kind of thing someone would do in a Jules Verne novel."

I still hadn't had a chance to talk to Nas about how Rose was actually nice, just like I thought she'd be. Before yesterday, she hadn't really talked to anyone from seminar but now it felt like she, Nas, and I were a group.

I sat down in my usual chair and tilted it back, with my hands behind my head. "Thanks, Rose. Exactly. So, now we just wait for him to come through that door quoting some passage from *Twenty Thousand Leagues* and I stand up all sure of myself and tell him I demand satisfaction."

Nas still looked skeptical. "He might kick you out twice."

"Just wait."

And so we did. It was a few minutes past nine, which was weird, because Bessier was never late. But maybe his oddball book club had been out partying the night before.

But at twelve minutes after nine, he still hadn't arrived. Then a younger woman who I'd seen in the collège's main office came into our class.

"Attention, élèves!" Everyone turned their focus to her as she spoke in extremely fast French—way too fast for me to understand—as some of my classmates gasped and exclaimed, "Mon Dieu," and "Quoi?" I heard Bessier's name a few times, so I knew it had to do with him, but when she finished, she was out of breath and didn't wait for questions. She swept out of the room as suddenly as she had come in.

I looked at Rose and Nas. "What did she just say?"

Rose's face was pale, and I thought of the car the night before. The chocolate croissant I'd eaten at breakfast spun around in my stomach. I was gladder than ever I'd taken the snails off my slice of pizza.

"Professor Bessier didn't show up for an early-morning conference, which he's never missed. So they went to his office and everything was a mess...."

"Which is for sure not like him," I said, thinking of his extreme tidiness. Also thinking of how, when I'd seen him leave, the office was still in order.

"Then the police were here because a witness said they saw a man being pushed into a car last night,"

Nas said. "And his book bag turned up by the side of a bridge—empty! They're saying foul play. No Bessier means class is temporarily canceled."

I'd figured out the no class until Monday part because so many of the other students had already started to file out of the room. They were chatting in French and I could make out that a lot of them didn't buy that anything had happened to Bessier, and they were enjoying the day off from class. And I got it: If not for what I'd seen the night before, I might have had a hard time believing Bessier was at the center of a crime. I'd probably think Bessier was fine and had forgotten to set his alarm because he'd spent too long painting one of his little divers.

But I'd seen too much and knew too much.

I grabbed Rose's and Nas's shoulders. "You need to come with me."

CHAPTER TWELVE

Things Don't Look Good for Bessier

THE DOOR TO BESSIER'S OFFICE WAS OPEN BUT CRISS-crossed with police tape. One peek inside was all I needed to see. The office was a disaster.

I ducked under the police tape, with Rose and Nas following behind me. Rose gasped, and Nas let out a sound that was a cross between a "whoa" and an "oh no," like "whoaano."

Papers were everywhere, and books had been tossed from the shelves. The desk drawers were pulled out and upended on the floor. The half-painted deep-sea diver Bessier had been working on was lying facedown on a pile of file folders that had been dumped from their wooden cabinet. This was not a fun post-party mess. This was a foul-play mess.

"Okay, I was here last night and it did not look like this."

"Why were you here last night?" Rose said.

"I wanted to see if he'd let me take the test."

"At first, I thought you were an American...clown," she said. "But you're very conscientious."

I shrugged. "I guess." But inside I was kind of proud that someone as smart as Rose thought I was a good student.

Nas wasn't paying attention to our conversation. He was peering at the papers on the ground and on Bessier's desk.

"Someone must have been looking for something," Nas said, stepping carefully over a hot-air balloon model that had been thrown from its display.

I thought of how Bessier had hidden my book in the secret compartment but traded it for one of his own.

"But what would Bessier have?" Rose asked. I already knew.

I crossed the small room and stood in front of the *Nautilus* model. I tried to move it, but it didn't budge. There had to be some kind of switch. The shelves surrounding the *Nautilus* were loaded with more of Bessier's

Jules Verne trinkets, and whoever had searched the office must have figured they were all junk, but I knew better. I started feeling around behind them, looking for some kind of switch to open the secret compartment.

"Owen, what are you doing?" Rose asked.

"Yeah, O, this is a crime scene," Nas said.

"There's a compartment back here, somewhere." I picked up a glass model of a blimp and set it down next to a ceramic rocket, then felt around on the shelf.

"I wonder how many flea markets Bessier had to search to get all this stuff," Nas said.

"Maybe you get a box of weird junk when you decide to be a Jules Verne expert," Rose joked.

"All this old stuff makes me nervous," I said. I tried lifting the submarine again, like Bessier had.

"Why is that?" Rose asked, joining me at the submarine. She gave it a little nudge but nothing happened for her, either.

I slapped the top of the model like I was ringing one of those old bells at hotel front desks. The blimp and the rocket teetered and then started to fall from the shelves above it. I stepped in front of Rose and threw myself under them, catching both before they hit the floor. Whew. Close call. "Because I worry about breaking everything," I said, grinning up at Rose and Nas.

They helped me up. Rose put a tiny dog in a space

helmet back inside its little toy ship. I found a spot for the blimp and set it back nicely. Nas and I fixed several glass octopuses that had tipped onto their sides. I checked out our work. "Good as new," I said, patting the wall next to the shelves very gently.

When I did, the whole wall of Bessier's junk started to fall. Divers and rocket ships and tiny astronauts and a set of Captain Nemo bookends all crashed to the floor.

"Oh no," I said. One of the Captain Nemo heads had broken off and was glaring up at me. For good reason. I'd decapitated him.

"Oh no is right," came a voice in French. An adult voice.

My stomach flipped because my first thought was that Bessier would never let me retake the test if he saw how I destroyed his Jules Verne stuff, even if some of it had been destroyed before I got here. But when I looked at the door, it was much worse.

The guy was younger than my mom or Bessier, with light brown hair that touched his shoulders but didn't do much of anything else, just hung there. He was rumpled looking, like he'd maybe slept in the teachers' lounge. His button-up shirt was wrinkled and had a galloping horse stitched on the pocket. And he wore cologne, way too much. Overall, he seemed to be trying very hard at whatever on-purpose messy look he was attempting to pull off.

He flashed a police badge and it all made sense. A plainclothes cop named Arthur Gagnon.

"What are you kids doing here?" he said in French. His mouth drooped in a frown and he had dark circles under his eyes. Officer Sadface was a better name for him than Arthur.

Rose screamed. A loud, pierce-your-eardrum, horror-movie scream. Officer Sadface jumped back, leaving just enough space for us to get through the doorway. "My life is ruined," Rose said. "I came here for the bake sale and there is no bake sale." She stomped her foot. Now Nas and I jumped back.

"What is this mess? Do you know Professor Bessier?" Rose ducked under the tape and said to him, smiling like she'd short-circuited, "This isn't the place for the extra-credit bake sale, Kids Help Kids project?" Rose picked up a shell painted on the inside with a scene from *Twenty Thousand Leagues*. She put it in her mouth and pretended to take a bite. "This is the worst cookie I've ever had! What kind of bake sale is this?"

Nas and I traded a look and then we chose two of Bessier's knickknacks—a miniature diving helmet for me and a moon model for Nas—and did the same. "You call this a cupcake?" I said.

"This cream puff is phenomenal, though," Nas said. He held it out to the cop. "Try some!"

The guy backed away like we were deranged.

"What are you talking about? You shouldn't be here! Do you know where Professor Bessier is?"

Rose grabbed me and Nas by the hands and pulled us toward the door. "I don't know who you are, but you're definitely not in charge of the bake sale," she said. Poor Officer Sadface's eyes widened like he was more nervous to be around Rose than we were around him. Rose had never acted like a spoiled rich girl the way Nas said she would. But in her nice clothes and with her outraged tone, she was now playing the part pretty well.

She dragged us past the cop and glared at him. "I'll be speaking to my advisors."

He ran a hand through his hair, looking confused. Maybe he was new at his job, but he clearly didn't know what to do as we brushed past him. But as I gave the office one last glimpse before we turned into the hall, I saw Bessier's green slippers peeking out from under his desk.

And now I knew what to do to get the book.

But first we had to run.

Rose led us to the end of the hallway and around the corner, where the corridor was even narrower. Along one brick wall was an alcove with a bench tucked into it. She flung herself within it, pulling Nas and me down with her. It took a second for us to realize we were all still holding hands and to let go.

After an awkward couple of seconds, Nas spoke. "Do you seriously have advisors?" he asked Rose.

She shrugged. "More like a staff," she said. "There are times when acting like a bratty rich girl is helpful, and that was one of them. Sorry if it was embarrassing."

"Are you kidding?" I said. "You kept that cop from arresting us, or something."

"He's probably looking for a bake sale now," Nas said.

"Hopefully he's not just in the office, trying to eat Bessier's stuff," I said. "Because we have to go back in. I think whatever happened to him happened because of that old book," I said. "And I know where he put it."

I crept to look at the hallway where Bessier's office was and saw no sign of the cop or anyone else. I signaled for my friends to follow me.

Rose stood watch by the door. Nas was two steps behind me as I pulled the pointy green slippers from under Bessier's desk.

I chucked off my Vans and slid my feet into the shoes. "Are you sure you should be trying on Bessier's shoes?" Nas said.

"Just trust me," I said, and left him standing in front of Bessier's chalkboard. I shuffled over to the *Nautilus* in Bessier's slippers. They were too big but still comfortable. At this point, Nas and Rose were staring at me like my skull had cracked in half and they could see all my brain goo.

I was forgetting something.

"Aha! The stance!" I said, more to myself than my friends. I set myself up like I was going to shoot a free throw. I bent my knees and went into a mini-squat, then tried again to lift the submarine.

Nothing happened.

"We don't need the book, O," Nas said. "Like, if Bessier is even alive, maybe he'll feel like he got a second chance at life and let you take the test anyway."

Rose whacked him. "But if someone foul-played Bessier for this book, why would we leave it for them to find? Owen is right."

I liked Rose saying I was right, and that she was thinking what I was thinking. Maybe we were just a bunch of middle-school kids, but we had found the book first, and something about the whole situation made me feel like I was supposed to have it.

But that would never happen if I couldn't open the vault. I kicked at the tiled floor, frustrated. Bessier's slipper caught in a triangle-shaped groove in the tile. There were two of them, about as far apart as you'd put your feet if you were a tall man squatting for a free throw.

"His shoes are a key!" I said. Maybe too loudly because Rose shushed me. And Nas had stopped paying

attention to what I was doing because he was staring at the weird writing on Bessier's chalkboard.

Rose stepped over a shattered model of Mars to peer at the floor with me as I lined up the pointy edge of the slippers with the two triangular slots in the tile. I squatted down, until I could feel the slippers almost click into place against the tile.

Now when I lifted the *Nautilus*, it was easy. The heavy brass submarine tipped right over to reveal the shelf containing my book. *La Prophétie de Jules Verne.* My book. As I took it out of the compartment, a last lone moon man statue wobbled and toppled to the floor. Hopefully, Bessier had backups.

"That was easy," I joked. Rose laughed quietly.

Nas didn't say anything, though. When we turned around, we saw that his head was tilted all the way to the side as he stared at the blackboard and the characters Bessier had written.

"Nasim," Rose said gently.

Startled, maybe by hearing his full name, he turned toward her. With his thumb, he pointed backward at the chalkboard. "Bessier's got some whack stuff going on, doesn't he?"

"Looks like it, but we need to go. Now," Rose said. "Before the police come back."

Nas snapped a picture of the blackboard on his

phone. I put the book under my arm and we turned to leave.

We crept out into the hallway, which was clear.

We took two steps before we heard the cop's voice behind us, turning the same corner from where we'd hidden earlier. "Not so fast."

"Yes, fast," Rose said. "Run!"

CHAPTER THIRTEEN

Getting Chased Again

I SHOVED THE BOOK UNDER MY SHIRT AND RAN ALONG-side Rose and Nas.

The cop was panting behind us and I wondered if he had asthma, too, or if he was just out of shape. Whatever was going on with his lungs, I was glad we could outrun him.

We burst out a side exit and onto the street along-side the school. I was still wearing Bessier's strange slippers. My Vans were in his office. I couldn't go back for them unless I wanted the cop to arrest me, but wearing pointy green shoes in public was definitely a fashion crime.

And, just to prove the slippers shouldn't be worn outside the professor's cluttered office, I tripped on one of the cobblestones and the book went flying, skidding across the ground.

"Hold on, you three. I have some questions," the cop puffed behind me.

"Owen, get up!" Rose grabbed my arm. "Nas, get the book!"

We scrambled to follow her orders as the cop got closer. I felt an asthma attack coming on and I shuffle-ran in the slippers while trying to get my inhaler out of my pocket.

"Get to that car," Rose said, pointing to a maroon town car idling just across the street.

Nas and I slowed down and looked at one another like we didn't know if we should do it. Maybe Rose was comfortable getting into sinister-looking cars, but it wasn't exactly my thing.

Rose skidded to a stop in front of the car and waved at us to run quicker.

The cop was gaining on us. "I guess it's our best option," Nas said, and we scrambled toward the creepy town car. My breathing was short and shallow but I didn't want to stop to use my inhaler. Rose yelled at the cop, "No time for questions, gotta run!"

"She's enjoying this too much," Nas said to me as

the door to the car popped open and he pulled me inside. Rose hurled herself in after us and slammed the door. I took a long, relieving hit off my inhaler and sank into the soft leather seat.

The driver nodded once but didn't say anything. "So, you're not a kidnapper, right?" I said, once my breathing got normal, because for all I knew, French kidnappers were silent and businesslike. Next to me, Nas still looked panicked, like someone had told him he'd be getting extensive and painful dental work with no novocaine. I thought I might look the same way.

"Your residence, Ms. Bordage?" The driver had a voice that sounded like he ate rocks for breakfast.

"Yes, thanks, Martin," Rose said, then leaned back against the leather seat and grinned. "Why do you guys look so stressed? That was fun."

CHAPTER FOURTEEN

What's in the Book?

I LEANED MY HEAD BACK AGAINST THE SEAT, JUST GLAD we didn't have to run anymore. About a mile from the collège, we came to a stop in front of a big brick building. It had at least a dozen steps up to a set of old-looking wood doors, and a wraparound balcony lined with stone gargoyles. It easily took up a whole block.

"I thought we were going to your house," I said. "Unless you think we're safer at this museum?"

Nas leaned closer to me and whispered, "I think this *is* her house."

If that was true, Nas had been wrong when he'd said Rose was from *one* of the richest families in France. Her family had to be *the* richest because this place was massive and important-looking. If Marie Antoinette had popped out onto the front steps in one of those giant ball gowns, it wouldn't have seemed out of place.

"And, it's kind of a museum," Rose said, rolling her eyes. "But my room is cool."

She thanked Martin and hopped out, racing up the front steps like it was no big deal to have the key to a castle. Nas and I followed behind her. Bessier's slippers made it hard to walk up steps, but it would be good to get indoors where no one could see me wearing them.

Inside, the place was like Bessier's office, except instead of there being so many collections cluttered everywhere, everything here was set up well, probably by someone who'd been paid a lot to do it. There was old stuff, but nice old stuff, not the kind of junk my mom bought at yard sales back home. The entry was covered with framed sepia-tone maps from around Paris, and as you walked farther inside, there were shelves displaying bronze seafaring instruments, golden clocks, and colorful glass perfume bottles. The furniture all looked like it had been stolen from a palace hundreds of years ago, but polished that morning. Rose led us down a hallway that was covered in gold-framed mirrors that made me feel like an old dead king was going to wander out and yell at us.

"Wait here," Rose said. "I'll get you some of my brother's old shoes."

Nas looked down at the slippers and laughed. "I don't know, Rose. I think Owen's making a statement." I rolled my eyes.

Rose laughed and jogged up a winding staircase to, I guessed, her brother's room.

"This place is nuts," I said to Nas as Rose disappeared. "Nice nuts, but I'm really scared I'll break something."

"Yeah, you're good at breaking stuff," Nas said.

"Shut up," I said, and gave him a friendly shove.

"Don't worry," came a voice behind me. "Everything is well insured."

I spun around and saw a tall woman with short dark hair and red lipstick. She was barefoot and in jeans—kind of baggy jeans that slouched on her in a cool way. She looked how I'd picture a cool French mom to look, like someone who put on an old record that wasn't terrible while she cooked dinner. This had to be Rose's mom.

Rose came down the stairs holding some shoes, and the woman gave her a light hug.

Rose didn't really hug her back. Instead, she held out the shoes to me and said, "I think these will fit. My brother's outgrown them."

The shoes she gave me would fit, or I would make sure they did, because they were a super-rare pair of custom Bête Noire high-tops. It was the best French skateboard deck manufacturer, and all my friends in the States wanted one of their boards. Most people didn't even know the company made shoes.

"Thank you," I said to Rose, and my voice cracked a little. She pretended not to hear and waved me off. She turned to her mom. "This is Owen and Nasim, from my seminar. We're going to go study."

A slight frown crossed the woman's face. "I thought class was canceled today." How did she know that, I wondered. Did French summer schools have a PTA? This lady didn't look like a PTA mom.

Rose shrugged. "You know how schools are. They want us to keep a routine."

"I remember school," the woman said. She smiled at me and glanced at the book, which Nas had handed off to me when we arrived. For a second, it almost seemed like she'd seen the book before, but maybe I was just being weird after the morning. "Well, you go study, and I'll make you some of my frozen hot cocoa. Secret recipe."

"Great," Rose said, like she wasn't impressed.

"Excellent," Nas and I both said, like we were.

Rose headed down the hallway and we followed. "Secret recipe frozen hot cocoa?" Nas said.

"Your mom is really nice," I added.

Rose shook her head as she opened the door to her room. "That's not my mom. That's Chantal LaForge. She's in charge of my dad's collections. And she curates the Musée des Arts et Métiers. Don't even mention Jules Verne to her, by the way. She'll never shut up."

We followed her inside. Rose's room was gigantic, like a hotel suite. The furniture was a mix of fancy old stuff and more modern things, and her walls were covered with posters from action movies and pages torn from French fashion magazines.

It was also big enough for a couch larger than the one at the apartment Mom and I were renting. Rose's couch was a deep purple, and I knew it would be extra comfortable. Rose flopped into a beanbag chair on the floor. She made a gesture like, "sit anywhere," and Nas and I both picked the couch. Right away, I kicked off Bessier's slippers and I put on the Bête Noires. They fit perfectly. I admired the metallic black crown logo on their sides.

"Anyway," Rose said, "my dad thought it was a big coup to get LaForge to take care of his stuff. My dad is always collecting interesting things and people. Plus, she's definitely his girlfriend. He thinks I don't know."

I think Nas and I could tell that Rose wasn't in the mood for questions or comments about how great LaForge seemed, so I set the book on a couch cushion

85

between Nas and me. "Let's see what this is all about."

I ran my hand over the cover, because it seemed like what they'd do in a movie. I read the gold-embossed title again.

"I should have noticed right away that this book is called *La Prophétie de Jules Verne*. Not an anthology," I said. "But have you ever heard of *La Prophétie*?"

Rose shook her head and pulled a laptop off the bed. "I know he wrote lots of books," she said, typing. "But I haven't heard of that one. And neither has Google."

Now Nas flipped the book over. The back cover was blank. No summary of what was inside, like on a modern book. "So, maybe it's like a book no one knows about? Like, we discovered something?"

The shiny golden tip of Bessier's slipper—the part that had unlocked the secret compartment—glinted at me from where I'd kicked it off. "That might explain his freak-out." What I didn't say was, if no one knew about it, why had Bessier hidden it and put a decoy book in his bag?

Rose's door tilted open and Ms. LaForge came in carrying a tray of frosted mugs. "Working hard, I see," she said, setting down the tray on a piece of colorful fabric that was on top of Rose's nightstand. "I made it extra chocolatey today."

Nas and I each took one of the mugs and thanked

her. My first sip gave me brain freeze but then the mega-chocolatey taste hit me. It was way better than normal hot cocoa, and way better than the green juice my Connecticut friend Evan's mom tried to serve us, but I wanted to get back to the book. As we drank, LaForge kind of lingered. She was staring at the book. "What a beautiful book. Is that your reading for the weekend?" she asked. "Hmm, *La Prophétie*? I've never heard of it."

Rose, who hadn't taken a delicious chocolate sip of her drink yet, gave her a tight smile. She stood up so that she was between LaForge and the book. "It's an art project. Not a real book," she said. "Just our idea of one."

"Very creative!" Ms. LaForge said. I couldn't tell if she believed Rose or not.

"Why'd you lie about the book?" I whispered after LaForge walked away. "What if she knows something about it?"

"Because it's your book and she would be a pain about it," Rose said. "Like, want it for her museum or something."

"Is that a bad thing?" Nas said.

Rose shrugged. She looked around her room. Her very nice room. "One thing I hate about my father having money is that he always wants one more thing, and he can always get it. I feel like LaForge is that way with her curation. She's always trying to find one more thing for her collections."

"And you don't want to share?"

"Not really. And I don't want it to be just another thing my father has collected and would like for LaForge to take care of for him," she said. But then she flipped open the book and scanned its pages. She didn't want to talk about her dad or LaForge.

"Okay, let's see what this thing is all about." Nas and I bent forward on the couch to view what Rose was looking at.

There were several blank pages, and then finally, a page with words, in French.

"To the ones who've found my book, welcome," it began.

It's no mere accident you hold in your hands my prophecy. Only readers with a sense of adventure would be granted the right to these pages. What lies within are more than clues but keys to adventure, wonder, and possibly treasure. The only thing I ask is that you do not skip ahead. When I devise a quest, I want my readers to remain in suspense, so follow these pages

in order and may your journey reveal great
things!

Jules Verne

"Whoa, do you think that's really his signature?" I
said.

"I wonder how much that's worth," Nas said.

"Maybe we *should* show this book to your...to Ms.
LaForge," I said to Rose. "What if she can sell it for millions?"

"You guys! We have a book by Jules Verne that basically says it's a treasure map. Even if we don't find it, the
adventure should be *ours*, not LaForge's."

Nas and I gave each other a look. She wasn't going to
take "maybe later" for an answer.

"You're right," I said. There was a part of me that
was curious about the book and where it would lead us,
but why did Rose have to be such an overachiever and
get right to it?

On the page after the letter were a bunch of lines
of symbols, like someone broke off the tops of musical
notes and shook them up.

"That's the page Bessier was looking at when he was
writing on the board last night," I said. "Or I think it
is."

"Huh." Rose squinted as if that would make the

weird characters make sense. Nas tilted and bobbed his head like he was listening to a beat. We all stared at it as our frosty iced chocolates got to room temperature. Nas started drifting off to sleep, it seemed. Rose stood up from her beanbag, knocking the book off my lap. When it fell to the floor, a cloud of dust rose from the book's binding and went right up my nostrils. It must have gone up Rose's, too, because she made a dry coughing noise.

Then, at the same exact moment, we both covered our faces to sneeze loudly into our elbows.

Nas woke up in a frenzy. "What's going on?" Then, without even asking why Rose and I were sputtering out dusty breaths, he said, "And wait, I think I had a dream. Or something. Gimme the book."

He didn't wait for us to hand it to him. He grabbed it off the floor and opened to the page. Then he took out his phone.

"I think I know what Bessier was doing on his blackboard."

CHAPTER FIFTEEN

First Clue

Friday, June 19, 10:21 a.m.

NAS OPENED THE PICTURE HE'D TAKEN OF BESSIER'S BLACK-board on his phone. Then he held the picture next to the book for a few seconds. Rose and I watched as he squinted and twisted the photo, grumbling.

"Do you have a hand mirror?" Nas asked Rose.

"Um, no, I use my phone as a hand mirror," she said. "But there's that one." She pointed to the mirror over her dresser. It had a gold frame and seemed like a mirror that could whisk you to another dimension, but Rose's dresser was cluttered with more or less normal girl stuff: a framed picture of her and a couple of other girls, a tray with a bunch of earrings and rings scattered on it, and a phone charger.

Nas took the book from us and brought it over to the mirror. He held the page with the characters up to the glass.

"Come here," he said. He pointed at the reflection and at his phone. "They look like they go together. Like, see how the first one on the board looks like half a bow tie? So does the first one in the book, when it's reflected."

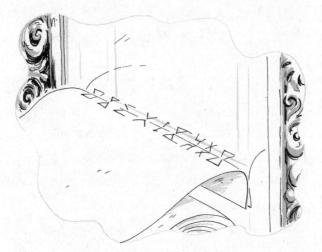

"Let's copy them down," I said. Rose already had a pen and notebook ready and gave them to me.

I'd just finished when Ms. LaForge knocked softly and came into the room again. "Does anyone want refills?"

Rose dropped one of her throw pillows over the book so LaForge couldn't see it. But she was staring at my notebook. "We're okay," she told LaForge.

She tilted her head slightly to the side and said, "Oh, using runes to tell your fortunes, hmm? How fun!" She headed back toward the door, adding, "Let me know if you need anything at all."

Rose rolled her eyes. I didn't get why Rose didn't seem to like her more. If her dad had to have a girlfriend, wasn't it good he picked someone who was so interested in her? I knew my mom loved me, but she was hardly ever home when I'd had friends over, let alone made us yummy treats.

I was about to ask Rose what the deal was, but she took the notebook from me and said, "Runes! I should have known. This is like the cryptogram at the beginning of *Journey to the Center of the Earth*."

"That's another book by Jules Verne, our next reading assignment," Nas said.

"Yeah, and I've read it already. Or my dad read it to me when I was little," Rose told him.

"Okay, but what are runes? Like, the Roman Colosseum?" I asked.

Rose shook her head. "No, *runes*, not ruins. They're like an ancient alphabet that dates back to probably the first century. They're symbols, and sometimes they can stand for a letter in the alphabet we use now, or sometimes they can stand for a thing, or a concept. Almost like a hieroglyph."

"But what do they mean?" I said.

"We won't know until we find out," Rose said. "We're going to the library."

When Rose said "library," I thought she meant a library near her house, not *in* her house. But of course her place had a library. A giant one, two doors down from her room. The ceiling was a stained-glass dome that looked like hundreds of open books, but there were no other windows, just massive dark wood shelves filled with dusty-looking volumes. It was like something out of a movie. A movie that had cost a fortune to make.

Rose pulled a thin book and a thicker book from the shelves. The first was a leather-bound copy of *Journey to the Center of the Earth* and the second was a thicker book of ancient alphabets. She handed that one to me. "I think there's a page of runic characters, somewhere near the middle." Then she smirked. "I always wanted to crack a code. Guess I got my wish."

She paged through the *Journey* book as Nas and I flipped past pages of strange characters until we got to runic ones.

The runic symbols looked like this:

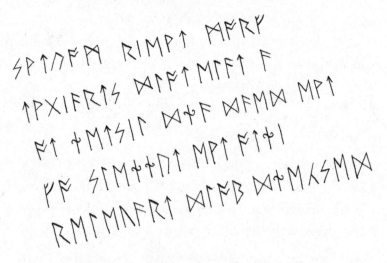

A lot like the letters we'd linked together.

"So, in *Journey*, there's a whole scene where the main characters Otto and Axel—Otto is this geologist who's obsessed with this old journal he finds that has instructions for reaching the center of the earth, and Axel is his nephew, who's just going along with it to impress a girl—discover a piece of runic writing that helps them to find the secret opening that will take them to the center of the Earth." She was reading a page and frowning. "It's a little complicated. Stuff about different languages and how many consonants each had and…We'll never figure it out!"

But Nas and I were already figuring out which letters matched which runic character.

"I think this might be slightly different," Nas said, looking over her shoulder. "We had the half letters and Bessier sort of cracked it. But it's definitely runic. When you line up the symbols, they match your runic book."

We each took a section and found the letter that corresponded to the symbol.

When we were done, it read, SHTUOM RIEHT MORF THGIARTS DLOT ELAT A OT NET-SIL DNA DAED EHT FO SLENNUT EHT OTNI RELEVART DLOB DNECSED.

"Makes no sense," Nas said.

I was starting to think we needed a seminar in using old books to find treasure. But then Rose whispered, "The mirror!"

"Duh, I can't believe I didn't think of that," Nas said.

I had no idea what they were talking about. Rose seemed to sense that and said, "We need to hold the code up to a mirror again, just like before."

"On reflection, that makes sense," I said. My friends groaned at my bad joke. Which kind of showed they were really my friends. But when I held the book up to an old, gold-framed mirror hanging above a writing desk in the library, the words still didn't make sense.

I studied the letters. Left to right...right to left, and then it hit me. "They're backwards!" I said. "Look, the first word is 'mouths.'" When we reversed the writing, the message read:

MOUTHS THEIR FROM STRAIGHT TOLD TALE A TO LISTEN AND DEAD THE OF TUNNELS THE INTO TRAVELER BOLD DESCEND.

"And the words are out of order, too. It's probably supposed to be addressed to the bold traveler," Rose said. She grabbed the paper from me and started to write. "See?"

Descend, bold traveler, into the tunnels of the dead and listen to a tale told straight from their mouths.

"That's it!" Nas said. "It has to be."

I still had questions. Or at least doubts.

Bessier was missing, and the first code of the book wanted us to talk to the dead. Chasing a ten-year-old had been one thing, but I wasn't up for a zombie encounter. And descending into tunnels couldn't be good for my asthma.

"Tunnels of the dead sounds like a terrible way to end the day," I said.

Fortunately, Nas agreed. "Yeah, there's no rule that says just because you transcribe a message from a weird old book you have to do what it says."

Rose slammed her book shut. "No, there's no rule that says we have to follow the path laid out for us in an old book. But we chased a kid through Paris and wound up in a strange store and now we have a book supposedly by Jules Verne leading to a treasure he may have hidden! Don't you think that means something?"

I knew she was right, but I couldn't help making a joke. "It means we should have gone to a different bookstore, maybe?"

Rose was pacing around the library now, and she didn't laugh at my joke. This time, it felt less friendly. "I think it means that we're lucky enough that a once-in-a-lifetime adventure landed in our laps, and you want to laugh it off. Play it safe if you want, but I'm going to figure this out. So, what do you think he meant by 'tunnels of the dead'?"

Stomping around in her combat boots, she was like some intense drill instructor in a flowered dress. She was also right.

"Maybe a cemetery?" I offered.

"Great," Rose said. "If there are two things France has more of than any other country, it's baguettes and cemeteries."

"And mimes," I joked.

This time, Rose laughed. Really loud. Maybe I could handle some dead stuff.

Nas hadn't said anything. I could tell he was thinking because his head was bobbing, as if he could hear a beat we couldn't. "I know exactly where the tunnels of the dead are."

CHAPTER SIXTEEN

Underground

Friday, June 19, 12:00 p.m.

"So, about two years ago, DJ Spindle played this underground Halloween party at the Catacombs," Nas said, once we were out on the street. After Rose's speech, we'd been in a rush to get on with the adventure. He looked sideways at me. I was on my board, riding slowly, with the book in a black messenger bag Rose had taken from her brother's room. "Owen, the Catacombs are these underground tunnel tombs filled with skulls, bones, and dead stuff."

"But why a tunnel? Aren't normal cemeteries creepy enough?"

"They're old mines," Rose said. "The cemeteries in the 1700s were overflowing. A wall even collapsed at one mass grave."

"Extreme dead guy pileup."

"So they got the mines ready and moved millions of bodies to them," Rose said. Like she was talking about someone opening a new Target. "Then later, hundreds of bones were dropped down there during the Revolution."

"Lovely," I said. "And now they throw parties there?"

"DJ Spindle did," Nas said.

"It's usually just visited by tourists and school field trips. I went when I was ten," Rose said. "But that party was probably the most actual French people to visit the Catacombs at one time in years. Besides the dead ones."

A street vendor who must have overheard Rose laughed and muttered something I didn't understand. "What did he say?" I asked.

"He said it's a tourist nightmare," Nas said. "It might be crowded today."

💀 💀 💀

"Crowded" turned out to be an understatement. Imagine the longest line you've ever seen at Disney World and then put six of them next to each other. "How are we going to do this?" I said. Rose's comfy couch and more of Ms. LaForge's iced cocoa were sounding really good compared to going into death tunnels with a sweaty mob.

Rose led us to the end of the line. "The book has been waiting for who knows how long. I think we can stand in line for a little while."

Nas had his head bent over his phone. "It says here that in busy months, it's a good idea to buy your tickets in advance. Or even better, to get a jump-the-line pass. Oh, but that's expensive."

As if to prove what he was saying, a guide leading a group of well-dressed tourists passed by us. They didn't look half as tired and exasperated as everyone waiting in line, and they caught some dirty looks from a mom who was clutching a kid screaming, "I want ice cream, not skulls!"

Rose frowned. "I think we're stuck here today," she said. "It will move fast."

It did not move fast. Fifteen minutes later, we were only a few steps from where we started.

"So, what do you both normally do in the summers here?" I asked them.

"If my parents don't have to work, sometimes we drive out to a place in the countryside. It's not fancy," Nas said. "But we know the lady who owns it and she goes to visit her sister in Belgium. The internet is awful there, and my parents love that."

"Rough," I said.

"It's not the worst. It's a little boring at first, and then you get used to it."

"What about you?" I asked Rose. I knew she probably went on amazing vacations.

"My father and I go down to the Riviera. It's beautiful but he still works every day. I end up reading by the beach most of the time," she said. She shrugged. "He's promised to take me somewhere I really want to go but there's never time."

"Where do you really want to go?" I asked.

"The States, actually," she said. "Maybe the Jersey Shore."

"Are you serious? My mom's taken me there! It's pretty corny," I said. "I'm sure the Riviera is nicer."

"Corny sounds more fun," Rose said.

"Yeah, one year my mom kept giving me money so I could win this giant stuffed goldfish you got by throwing rings around milk bottles," I said. "I was so bad at it, and those games are rigged. The guy working the booth finally felt sorry for us and just gave me the fish."

103

"See? That would never happen on the Riviera. What did you name it?"

"Floaty. But I was seven," I said. "I haven't been there in a long time. Right about now, I'd probably be at my friend Darren's house. He has a pool."

"That sounds way better than going…" Nas checked his phone again. "Twenty meters underground to see if there's treasure in a big cave of bones."

I shook my head. "I'm having a great time." It was true. Much as I liked my friends back home, I couldn't imagine any of them getting charged up to go on an adventure like this one. Sure, waiting in line for a tourist attraction wasn't adventurous on its own, but there was something exciting about being the only people in line who were going into the Catacombs in hopes of finding treasure.

We bought water and popcorn from vendors selling snacks to people waiting to get inside, and finally after more than two hours, it was our turn to go inside. Rose had bought us tickets on her phone, and the attendant scanned the screen and directed us to wait in a group with a few families who were also about to descend.

The entrance was arched and made of metal, with the faces of an angel and a demon embossed into it. Old green paint peeled off it in places, making the faces look like they were melting. Basically, it was not a door you even wanted to knock on, much less open.

Our tour guide was explaining the rules—photos were okay, touching or making rubbings of the inscriptions was not—but I couldn't stop staring at the faces along the entry.

Even the little kid who'd wanted ice cream and not skulls seemed less nervous than I was, so I took a deep breath as the guide led us inside. The cool, damp air was nice after being outside for so long, and it wasn't as dark as I thought it was going to be.

Then we got to the staircase. It spiraled down and the guide said it was 131 steps. "You guys really didn't want the dead to have an easy time getting back to the surface, huh?"

Rose rolled her eyes. "Come on," she said, following our group as we took the steps slowly down.

"Does anyone think we've been descending an awfully long time?" I said.

"It *was* an old mine, remember?" Rose said. "They need to go very deep."

Our group crouched under an archway with a stone tablet above it. In big, threatening letters, it said:

Arrête! C'est ici l'empire de la mort

"Does that mean what I think it means?" I asked.

"If you think it means 'stop! Here lies the empire of the dead,' then yes," Rose said. I got a chill. My French friends were much more comfortable with death than I was. Maybe because they took field trips to underground tombs, and back in America, my class had gone to an apple orchard.

Once we crossed under the archway, Rose said, "Well, at least there are no more steps."

Here was a long, narrow tunnel, lined with bones. Imagine all the bones you can and then multiply those bones by a thousand. That many bones. A lot of them were skulls, which somehow seemed worse than basic leg and arm bones because you knew they were human bones.

Nas groaned. "Doesn't it feel like some of them are watching us?"

"With what eyes?" Rose joked.

"You're not helping."

We stood in the tunnel, looking around as our tour group took photos and posed with skulls behind them. The ice cream kid had completely changed gears and was way into the bones. Good for him.

We passed more etchings on the walls. Some of them had dates and streets. "Those are the names of the cemeteries they moved down here," Rose explained. She stopped at one. "Les Innocents was the biggest cemetery in the city and the rotting bodies smelled so bad that street performers didn't want to work anywhere near it. They moved the bodies down here."

While it didn't smell awful in the Catacombs, it didn't necessarily smell good.

Ahead of us, we could hear the slight murmur of tourists in groups that had left before ours. I had the feeling that we weren't going to find any treasure here.

"When did they first start letting the public come here?" I asked Nas and Rose. I was trying to figure out a long quote in Latin from someone named Horace that was engraved on the wall. Unfortunately, my Latin was way worse than my French. As in, I didn't know any.

"It opened for VIPs in the early 1800s and then more widely in 1874," Rose said. She really paid attention on her field trips.

"Guys, I don't think Jules Verne would have hidden treasure right in the middle of a tourist attraction. There must be another room, or path, he would have taken."

"The fancy tours sometimes go into other areas," Nas said.

"I have an idea," I said. "Follow my lead and don't freak out."

Then I started to gasp like I was having an asthma attack. "Help," I wheezed at the tour guide. "I need to get out of here. I'm having…an…attack."

The tour guide's eyes bugged out. "Oh no…," he said. He took me by the arm. "Are you okay?"

"I will be if I can leave. Point me the fastest way."

The tour guide gathered Rose, Nas, and me together and said, "It'll be faster to take the less-used routes." He pointed toward a small curved door. "Go through there and the left tunnel will lead you to join the tours that skip the line. Then you cut through and take the staircase at the end that leads up."

"Thank you, sir," Rose said. She'd caught on to what I was doing.

I nodded and suddenly felt bad about using my asthma as a prank. I zipped ahead of my friends in the direction he'd sent us. Inside the small door was a passage that led left. The tunnel was dimly lit and we could hear voices from a tour group ahead. But a passage on the right was roped off. The tunnel beyond it was very dark in a way that made me sure it led to more dark.

"That's where we need to go," I said.

"You're kidding, right?" Nas said.

"I think he's right," Rose said. "No one could have hidden something where hundreds of people walk every day."

We heard voices. Probably another group coming. "Let's go now, before we get caught." I hopped the rope ahead of my friends and was plunged into darkness. Nas and Rose made it over the rope, and we stumbled into one another as our eyes adjusted.

Quietly, we took small steps in the tunnel, which was tighter than the previous one. I was able to see ahead of me, but not far. This part of the Catacombs was mostly brick, with some Latin words here and there.

A scratching noise came from somewhere behind us. "Did you hear that?" I asked.

"Probably just a rat," Nas said.

"Rats?" I said. I'd seen *Ratatouille*, I knew Paris had them, but in Connecticut, we had more mice than rats. How big could a rat get if it lived under Paris in a tunnel of bones? I could only imagine.

Rose waved us onward. "We need to keep moving if we ever want to get out of here."

She and Nas walked farther into the darkness, and I rode my skateboard slowly on the stone floor. Now I was glad to have brought it, so that my feet weren't directly touching the ground. I really, really hated the Catacombs.

I still felt lousy about faking an asthma attack. That guide had seemed really worried. I tried to focus only on what was right in front of me, so I wouldn't panic about how much longer we'd be down here. I skated a few feet ahead of Rose and Nas as we turned a corner, the bricks becoming bones again. I kept my arms as close to my body as I could so they wouldn't touch anything. I wondered if we'd misread the clue. Or if it even was a clue. Wasn't it possible the book was someone's idea of a joke?

My board hit a bump and I stumbled off, kicking what I thought was a rock that had gotten in my path. But, nope, it was a chunk of a bone. I wasn't sure what bone. Did it even matter? It's best not to get into specifics when you're skating over SOMEONE'S BONE.

When I got up, Rose was in something like a staring contest with a skull's empty eye sockets, as if she thought the clue would be there. I was giving up hope and wondering if we misread the runes. But above the skulls was another inscription. Not in Latin. This one was in French.

CHAPTER SEVENTEEN

A Dead Man's Game

I POINTED UP AT THE WORDS ETCHED IN THE STONE ABOVE the wall of skulls. "Those words...do you think..."

"Vos morts parlent tranquillement," Nas read. I knew *mort* was "dead," and *parler* was "speak...."

"Your dead speak quietly," I translated. "Wait a second! That's like the line from *Twenty Thousand Leagues*, except in the book it's 'Your dead sleep quietly'!"

"You really do know the book well. Bessier should have let you take the test," Nas said. But I didn't tell him it wasn't just about knowing the book. It was this feeling I had.

"Do you think these are the dead whose mouths he meant?" Rose said.

"Okay, but do you hear that?" Nas said.

We listened. This time, there were no scratching sounds. "I don't hear anything," I said.

"Exactly, because they're not talking!" Nas threw up his hands. "We need a tale from the mouths of the dead. But the dead can't speak!"

"You're being too literal," Rose said. "Maybe we have to reach inside the mouths to get the story."

"Oh, and that's not literal?" Nas said.

"So, I hear you guys bickering, but you're both missing the point," I said. "Which is, I'm not reaching in any of these mouths!" Even if I had a feeling about the inscription, there were some things I did not want to do. At all.

"We can all do it together," Rose said, patting my shoulder. It was nice. Not nice enough to make me want to feel around in a three-hundred-year-old's mouth, but nice.

"I hate group projects," Nas said.

Rose ignored him. "Everyone take a skull. Feel around inside for a clue, or a…something," she said. Then, with her eyes closed, she poked her fingers inside one of the skull's mouths.

"I played this game at a birthday party once," I joked. Rose and Nas laughed but I could tell we were all thoroughly creeped out.

"Oh, I don't like this," Nas said.

Rose rolled her eyes. "I doubt the person whose skull you're touching had these hopes for their afterlife, either."

Nas looked like he'd eaten a bad batch of chicken nuggets as he continued to search inside his. "What if their last meal got stuck in their teeth and I pull out thousand-year-old spinach?"

"Just don't think about it," Rose told him. She glared at me. "Nasim and I are doing our part. Come on, Owen. Choose a skull, any skull."

"Here goes nothing." I picked one of the skulls on the wall with the most dangly jaw, so my hand could almost slide in without touching bones. Then...

"Ahhhh! Noooo! It's got me," I screamed. "Help! It's alive!"

"Grab him!" Nas said, pulling my shoulders back.

"Don't fight too much, it might rip his arm off!" Rose said.

"Guys, I'm joking." I was trying not to laugh too hard at their terrified faces because it was nice to know they'd save me if I were in real trouble.

"Owen!" Rose was annoyed, but I could tell she thought I was funny. "Maybe you *are* just an American clown."

I tapped around inside what had once been some guy's head. "Wait, there's something here," I said, excited.

"Don't mess with us, O," Nas said.

"I'm serious! Let me get it." What I felt was a lump on the inside of the mouth, where the two halves of the jaw met. I pulled at it and it came loose. Like a rock, or a gem or something. I pulled out my hand. It was pink and smooth.

"That looks like old gum," Nas said. I gagged.

"I don't think that was from Jules Verne." Rose said. By now, she had gone through about a dozen skulls while Nas and I had only done a couple. "This is a bust. There's nothing here."

"I'm going to put this back in case he wants it." I started to reach back into the mouth, thinking I at least had a cool story for my What I Did This Summer essay, when I noticed a small letter *K* painted just below my skull's lower set of teeth.

"Look at this!"

"It's one letter," Nas said, peering over my shoulder. "What good does a *K* do us?"

"Here's another one!" Rose pointed at a skull just above her head. "A *P*!"

Nas crouched to look at a skull near my elbow. "Hey, yeah, this is an *I*," Nas said.

Not all the skulls had letters but a few did.

A skull with another letter *K* painted beneath the mouth protruded out farther than the rest. Its empty eye sockets seemed to stare right into my soul, so I turned my head to the side as I reached out and palmed it like a basketball. Then, as I tried not to think about whose head bone I was holding, I wiggled it.

It moved, as if it were on a track, leaving an empty slot. I reached over Rose for the skull that had been above it, with the *P* painted on it, and moved it down into the space. "It's like one of those puzzles, where you try to put the letters in order."

I started to shift other skulls, seeing if I could unscramble them into something like a word. There were twelve painted skulls in all.

E-R-I-K-A-D-R-K-P-N-A-C

"What if we figure out what they're supposed to spell first, and then move them?"

"There are two *K*s," I said. "Is there a Jules Verne character with two *K*s?"

Rose seemed to be mentally flipping through flash

cards she stored in her brain. "Captain Nemo's real name...Prince Dakkar!"

We began to slide skulls this way and that, not even paying attention to the fact that we were touching parts of very dead people, until finally the skulls spelled *Prince Dakkar*.

For a few seconds, nothing happened. It gave me

enough time to look at my palms and see they were coated in a light dust. Dead person dust...

Yuck. Rose and Nas must have noticed the gray stuff on their own hands, and we all started to wipe our palms on our clothes, almost missing that the word-puzzle skulls were fusing closer together with a grinding noise.

A portion of the skull wall swung inward, like a door opening into the wall. An opening leading to an even more claustrophobic staircase.

"More stairs," I said.

"What do we do?" Nas said.

"Go down them, of course," Rose said. "Owen, you can go first, since you're a guest in France."

"Oh, thanks," I said. I inched out onto the top step. This set of stairs was the darkest one yet. "Has anyone in this country ever heard of a night-light?"

Rose and Nas shuffled down the steps behind me. Nas had his hand on my shoulder and Rose had her hand on his as we crept down the staircase in an awkward human train. My foot slid on one of the steps and I had to grab for the wall, causing Nas's face to slam into the back of my head, and Rose to yelp as she missed the step.

"I'm sorry," I said. "I can't see down here."

"Duh, why didn't I think of it before?" Rose said. She must have taken out her phone and turned on the flashlight, because within a few seconds, the tight cavern was filled with light.

Under my sneakers, I could now see, weren't stairs. Or not stairs made out of stair material. I gagged a little. "Those are…"

"Bones," Nas said. "We're walking on dead people!"

The whole staircase was bones. Definitely human. Maybe tibias or fibulas, but in any case, a whole bonanza of bones.

"The tourists never get to see this," Rose said behind us. Something cracked under her foot.

"Eww," Nas said.

"We can turn back if you really want to," Rose said. "But we made it this far."

The tip of my sneaker got caught between a gap in two femurs laid next to each other. "No, we should keep going," I said. "I guess it's better than walking on living people."

When we'd first stepped into the Catacombs, the air had been colder than out on the summer streets, but it was warmer in the narrow passage, and stuffier.

"Maybe we're near the center of the earth," Nas said. "Doesn't it get warmer down there?"

But before I could say something about needing AC, we reached a stone chamber with a large coffin inside it.

"This seems really far down for a crypt," Rose said. "Usually they're right beneath a church."

She aimed the light from her phone around the corners of the dark cavern, looking for another path to follow, but there weren't any. The crypt was our final destination.

Every mummy, zombie, and vampire movie I'd ever seen made me sure this was a bad idea, but I knew what we had to do. I pointed at the coffin. "I think what we're looking for might be in there."

Nas looked like he'd eaten snail pizza.

"Let's just hope it's not a who."

CHAPTER EIGHTEEN

We Find Something

AFTER REACHING YOUR HAND INTO SKULLS, MOVING THE lid off a coffin doesn't seem as scary. It was heavy, though.

We pushed against the stone lid, getting it to move a half inch or so each time. Clouds of dust puffed around our faces. Something else skittered near my sneakers. I decided not to try to figure out what it was.

Finally, we had the lid shoved far enough back to see what was inside. Or who. Because of course it was another skeleton. But this one was wearing a navy captain's jacket and a cap. You'd be surprised how much less scary a skeleton is when it has a costume on.

Rose had a hand over her mouth. "There's something around its neck," she said in a muffled voice. Tangled in the skeleton's neck, or really, its very exposed vertebrae, was a chain with a medallion looped onto it. The medallion part, without a chest to rest on, had dropped down inside the skeleton's rib cage.

"Do you think it's a clue?" Nas said.

"I don't know. We should look at it," I said.

He shook his head. "I don't want to touch it."

If I just closed my eyes and grabbed it, we could be done here. It would be like pulling off a Band-Aid.

So, I reached in, right into the skeleton's ribs. I tried not to think about how they'd become ribs—that there'd been skin there once. Had Jules Verne thought this thing through? Had he known this dead guy or chosen a recently deceased random person to wear this necklace?

"Worst game of Operation ever," I said as I fumbled around inside the rib cage.

I finally felt the medallion and pulled, thinking I'd have to snap the chain to get the necklace off. Because no way was I getting any closer to Captain Bones to neatly unclasp the chain. But then I had it, chain and all. It must have been draped over the skeleton. Maybe whoever had buried him hadn't wanted to get that close, either.

I opened my eyes and stared at the golden medallion.

121

I had a piece of treasure. A clue. It felt great. Better than any boss battle. I'd never admit it to Rose, though.

I turned to my friends and held up the medallion against my chest to show Rose and Nas. I was about to ask, "What do you think? Is it me?" when something fell. From the sound of it, something bigger than even a large rat could push.

From above came a cracking noise, and the sound your shoe makes when you run on gravel, but ten times louder.

Then a brick came loose from the archway in front of us and smashed to the ground. Then another one.

"This isn't good," I said.

The giant stone coffin started to slide as the ground beneath it began to give way.

"We have to get out of here," Nas said.

I held tight to the medallion in my hand as we made for the exit.

"Are we sure that's what we came here for?" Rose asked. She leaned toward the coffin, almost putting her head inside as she gripped its outer edge. Bricks and stones from the crypt were raining down around us, forcing Nas and me to cover our heads and dodge them.

"Rose," I yelled. "Come on." Rose was frozen. She clutched the coffin as the floor beneath her rattled.

Then, with a giant breaking sound, the coffin slid farther away from her. She was stretched with one hand on the coffin and her feet on the ground, as the coffin crashed through the floor, pulling her forward. She let go, jumping toward us, but the floor under her feet cracked and splintered.

CHAPTER NINETEEN

More Adventure Than I Bargained For

ROSE SCREAMED AND GRABBED AT A BROKEN WOODEN plank that jutted out from the hole where the stone floor had collapsed. "Help me!"

Nas gripped the half of the crypt's brick archway that hadn't collapsed and reached out his arm to me. I clung to it with one arm and stretched my other arm out to Rose, but before she could latch on, the board she was holding cracked partway and she skidded farther into the hole. It was some kind of shaft beneath the crypt. Was it a booby trap?

"I can't reach," Rose said.

That was obvious. But if we took any more steps toward her, the whole place might cave in.

"Your board," Nas said, really quietly, like he was worried the floor would give way. He nodded at my skateboard, which, in all the excitement, I'd dropped. It was balanced on the board Rose was holding with a white-knuckled grip.

I crouched as carefully as I could and pinched my skateboard with the tips of my fingers. I extended it toward Rose, making my reach longer. Rose lifted one hand off the broken wood and stretched the slightest bit forward. The wood snapped with a horrible cracking sound. She gritted her teeth and heaved herself upward. If this didn't work, she'd fall into who knew what. I stopped breathing as she barely got hold of my deck. I adjusted my grip on the board so I could hold it with all my strength, wishing I'd tried harder at the pull-ups we did in gym class.

Nas pulled on my shoulder, helping me yank Rose and the board toward us.

A brick fell from the arch, right next to Nas's foot. "We don't have much time," he said.

"My shirt is caught," Rose yelled. The end of the long black T-shirt she had on over tights and a skirt was twisted on the splintered wood. We pulled hard, and Rose flew toward us, landing on her face between us. Her shirt had tears in several places.

"Sorry about your shirt," I said. Understatement apology of the century to make to someone who'd almost fallen down a mine shaft.

"Whatever, let's go!" she said, wiping dust from her eyes. We scrambled to our feet and sprinted for the bone stairs. We paused to catch our breath and looked back toward the crypt.

The foot end of the coffin was peeking out from the hole in the ground, when another snapping sound startled us, and the entire coffin vanished. A few seconds later, we heard a loud boom as the stone coffin must have hit the ground far beneath the crypt.

"That fall would have ripped a lot more than my T-shirt," Rose said. Then, more seriously, she looked from me to Nas. "Thanks for making sure that wasn't me."

"All for one, and one for all," I said.

"*Three Musketeers.* Different French author," Rose corrected me.

"And we got the clue," Nas said.

Forgetting we'd almost just died, I was about to pull out the medallion to show them. Then my stomach lurched as the step we were standing on dropped into the ground.

"The bone stairs are collapsing," Nas said. "Run!" We leaped away from the bottom stairs as they buckled beneath us, sprinting up the rest of the steps as they also toppled into whatever was below us.

We kept running, out the skull-puzzle door and into the closed tunnels, not even paying attention to where we were going. I had my board under my arm, and the medallion clutched in my hand. The bag with the book banged against my hip while we ran. I slid the medallion into my pocket so it didn't get caught on anything in our rush.

"This way," Nas said, turning down a corridor. We were in what must have been the employee tunnel. I smashed into a mop and bucket, skidding on the soapy water. But ahead of us, it seemed to narrow into darkness.

"Where are we even going?" I yelled.

"Away from the collapsing pile of bones," Nas said, waving me to go faster.

I knew he was right, but I had the feeling something was following us. Not a rat. I glanced back and thought I glimpsed a shadow flicker at the far end of the corridor. I shook it off. I was imagining things.

But still, I picked up my pace, trying to catch up to Nas and Rose, who I couldn't see anymore. I slammed into Nas's back in the dark. "Ouch," he said, tripping forward and knocking into Rose, who screeched and stumbled.

Suddenly, there was light. We'd fallen through a small door, like dominoes. My hand was on Nas's back and his hand was on Rose's shoulder and we splattered into a hallway. "Ouch," Nas said. "Why can't we land on anything soft?" We were covered in cobwebs and dust.

"We have to keep moving," Rose said, shaking her head so that dust spewed from her long hair. "I think this is the main level now. Let's go."

I wiped my face with my hand and came away with a palm coated in dust. "Is there a Catacomb locker room with showers?" I asked Nas.

"No jokes. We need to get out of here," Rose said. "You go first, Owen. Just keep the medallion safe. We'll be right behind you."

CHAPTER TWENTY

Stop Taking My Stuff

LOOKING LIKE A VERY FASHIONABLE ZOMBIE WEARING A lot of dust and the Bête Noire sneakers, I took off on my board, rolling down the length of the final passage of the Catacombs. The stone floor was bumpy and my stomach leaped around under my ribs, but I was making good time. The tunnel was pretty clear, just a few tourists listening to tour headsets. But as I turned down the exit corridor, I had to flip up my board. It was packed.

Rose and Nas were running and caught up to me as Rose shouted, "Move! Move! He's about to vomit! He mixed snails and McDonald's." She'd never let that first day at collège go. But it worked. The tourists stepped

aside as I made a dramatic show of grabbing my stomach and moaning. I didn't feel as bad faking a stomachache as I had the asthma attack, partly because after touching all those skeletons, I *was* a little nauseous.

I was close to the stairs that led out to the grounds around the Catacombs, trying to slip past two guys in Clippers jerseys tall enough to be players, and I couldn't hear Rose or Nas behind me anymore.

Then someone knocked into my shoulder from the opposite side. I stumbled against a woman ahead of me, who shoved me backward, and I felt the medallion slide from my pocket. My eyes swiped the floor, looking for the necklace. It wasn't there.

My face got hot with anger. All that work and some pickpocket had taken it?

Or, wait, *had* someone been following us?

I scanned the crowd in front of me. Then my eyes caught something shiny. The medallion was glinting in the hands of someone just ahead of me. I lunged and tried to grab it from the air. "Hey, that's mine," I said to the slender back of the thief, who wore a wide-brimmed hat and a purple coat.

I yelled, "You took my medallion!"

"Thieves are everywhere," said a man as he patted the wallet he had strapped across his chest.

Now I really felt like I would vomit. I had to get the medallion. I tore through the crowd, stumbling toward a glimpse of purple fabric ahead of me. I ran for it and saw it wasn't a coat, just a little girl's T-shirt.

"Stop! Thief!" I yelled, but no one was paying attention.

I shoved my way through the crowd and charged up the stairs. My lungs felt heavy and oatmealy again. I was outside and gulped for air but I couldn't get any. I dropped my board and reached into my pocket for my inhaler. I didn't have it. I must have taken it out at Rose's house. Which was unlike me. I never forgot my inhaler.

Then I saw a flash of purple again, creeping toward one of the ticket booths. It was the purple coat. And the thief. The medallion dangled from the thief's fingers as they held it out in front of themselves. Admiring it. I pushed as hard as I could, keeping my eye on the golden medallion sparkling in the sun. I was close, and the thief hadn't seen me. No way was I letting everyone in Paris take my stuff.

My legs burned and my side hurt and I couldn't breathe. I hurdled over a small dog and toward the golden pendant, toward the coated figure. They were inches away.

I needed air. I needed the medallion.

Air was definitely the priority. How had I gotten myself into this mess?

Then everything went black.

CHAPTER TWENTY-ONE

Help Arrives

SUNLIGHT WAS SEEPING IN THROUGH MY CLOSED EYELIDS, like it wanted to pry them open. I was lying down, but not in a bed, and I could hear voices around me.

A woman was saying, "Owen? Owen? Are you okay?"

I saw a blurred face and dark hair. Then I felt a cool hand on my forehead. My mom's hand? Had she come looking for me?

"Mo—" I started to say, until she came into focus.

It wasn't my mom. It was Madame LaForge. She was smiling down at me.

"Oh, thank goodness," she said. I sat up, remembering where we were as I saw the newly forming groups of tourists arriving at the ticket booths. "I've been look-ing all over for you."

She helped me to my feet, with her arm still around me. A woman and her husband stopped next to us and said to LaForge, "Is your son okay?"

Madame LaForge nodded. "He will be fine." It was kind of cool that she didn't correct them because I knew she wasn't trying to act like she was my mom, more that she didn't feel like talking to strangers when she was taking care of me. She passed me my inhaler. "You left this at the house. And when I saw your homework about the tunnels of the dead, I knew there could only be one place."

I pumped a burst of medicine from my inhaler into my lungs and felt more and more like I was okay to walk on the ground over the Catacombs, instead of being buried inside them. "I'm glad Paris only has one spot like this. It's really creepy," I said.

"I've always found it morbid, too," LaForge said. She was nice.

"Have you seen Rose or Nasim?" I asked LaForge. "They were with me down there."

I wouldn't tell her about the thief in the purple coat. I didn't want LaForge to think I was paranoid. And I didn't want her to call the cops, because they'd probably confiscate the book. Or worse.

"You must have had quite an ordeal," LaForge said, pulling a cobweb from my hair and inspecting it. I walked next to her as she headed for the door I'd come out of. "And some interesting homework."

"Thanks for coming to look for me," I said. "And bringing the inhaler."

"You fainted. Only for a few seconds and you seem to be okay now but please be sure to tell your mother," she said.

I thought she might hug me, but then Rose and Nas emerged with one of the tour groups. Rose had my skateboard. They spotted me but stopped short when they saw LaForge.

I waved my inhaler in front of them. "I left this at your house. And Madame LaForge..."

"Call me Chantal, please," she said.

"Chantal found it and our...homework...so she brought it to me. Which is good because I thought I was going to die."

Nas gave me a fist bump. "Yeah, it got dangerous down there."

"Because there were so many people," Rose said, jumping in before Nas could say any more.

Chantal put an arm around me and Nas. "I think you all could use a snack," she said. "And to clean up."

She set off a few steps in front of us. People smiled

at her as she passed. Madame LaForge was just one of those people everyone admired.

Rose nudged me with her elbow. "Did you see who was following us?"

I shook my head. "I passed out. I don't know what would have happened if Mad—Chantal—hadn't been there."

Now Nas whispered. "Did they get the necklace?"

The medallion. I'd forgotten about it. I'd been chasing the thief and I'd closed in and then I'd reached for it and…passed out.

"I…" I realized my left hand was clenched in a tight fist, and something solid and heavy was inside it. I must have grabbed it from the thief right before I passed out. And whoever had taken it wouldn't have tried to get it again with all the attention I must have attracted. I squeezed the medallion in my palm, not wanting to show my friends right here.

"Nope, we've got it," I whispered.

I slid the medallion back into my pocket.

CHAPTER TWENTY-TWO

An Invitation

Friday, June 19, 4:45 p.m.

ROSE'S HOUSE HAD SOME OF THE NICEST SHOWERS I'D ever used. I sort of wanted to stay under the warm water for as long as I could, because the medallion was stowed in the messenger bag, and Nas, Rose, and I would have to figure out what to do with it.

I kept thinking the same two thoughts, in a repeating cycle:

1. Someone was stalking us because they wanted the book, the medallion, or both.

And they probably weren't into using
friendly methods to get them.

2. The book had landed on my head, and I'd
gotten the medallion back, like we were
fated to have them and had no choice but to
see where this whole thing led us.

I wondered if Rose and Nas felt the same way. I finished my shower and dried myself off with a fluffy towel
that was heating on the rack just outside the shower.
Nice.

Rose had pulled some sweats out of her brother's
room—they were cool, of course, with a French graffiti
tag on the leg and arm—so I put them on and went down
the hall to Rose's room. Rose and Nas had cleaned off,
too, and were flipping through their phones. But they
didn't seem to be really looking at them.

When I walked in, they both jumped up. "Let's see
the medallion," Rose said.

On the way home, I'd put it in a pocket of the messenger bag with the book, and now I fished it out. I
held it out in my hand, and Rose and Nas huddled
around me. The medallion was small and heavy—it
was real gold, I thought—and it was embossed with a
shell design.

"What's that kind of shell called?" Nas asked,

reading my mind. The symbol looked familiar—it was a spiral, with a series of chambers inside. My favorite seafood restaurant back home—Peg Leg Patrick's—had a design like it on its menus.

Rose was already ahead of us, and she thumbed across a page on her phone. "Of course," she said. "It's a nautilus shell."

And then I got why the model in Bessier's office had the spirally front end....Captain Nemo's submarine, the *Nautilus*, was shaped like a nautilus!

"Do you think that's a clue?" I said. "We should check the book."

I was pulling the book from Rose's brother's bag

when someone softly knocked on the door. Madame LaForge—she wanted us to call her Chantal, but Rose called her LaForge so I didn't know how to think of her—slipped in, carrying a tray of small bowls filled with something cheesy and delicious-smelling. She was also wearing a long black dress and gloves that went up to her elbows. I pocketed the medallion before she saw it. Part of me would have loved to show her—if she really was a Jules Verne scholar, too, she'd probably be excited. But I knew Rose wouldn't want me to share our find.

"I thought you might need some comfort food," she said, and set the tray down. I was starving.

I managed to say thank you before picking up one of the small bowls and shoveling the warm, melty mixture into my mouth. LaForge watched us eat for a second. Rose might not have been a LaForge fan but she wasn't dumb. She wasted no time picking up a cup of the soup and plunging her spoon in. She didn't make any appreciative sounds like me and Nas.

LaForge was adjusting her hair in the mirror above Rose's dresser. Then she stopped. "You know, I have an idea." She smiled at me.

"I'm about to leave for the Musée des Arts et Métiers." I nodded, even though I had no idea what the musée was. I'd only heard of it when Rose said LaForge worked there. "Its collections are devoted to industrial design throughout the ages. We have everything from one of the first movie projectors to an early Mars rover. I'm the curator."

She rubbed her hands together with excitement.

"In fact," she continued. "We have an opening tonight. *Jules Verne: Inventor of the Future.* We've gathered many things Verne predicted in his work, long before they were invented. I'm surprised that your teacher didn't cover that. There's more ways to learn than hunched over books. I think you should all come, too."

I'd been thinking I should go home. "I just need to call my mom," I said, hoping that she'd tell me to come home.

"Of course," LaForge said.

I dialed and let it ring and ring. Mom sent a text as I waited for her to pick up: *Sorry, O, can't pick up. I'm about to give a lecture. I miss you! Be safe! Fun weekend soon!*

Okay, so that was that. I knew I could still go home and take a break, but my mom not even bothering to answer made me angry. She never invited me to anything she did at work. And LaForge had.

"I'm in," I said. "What should I wear?"

CHAPTER TWENTY-THREE
Not a Typical Friday Night

Friday, June 19, 6:00 p.m.

THE THREE OF US GOT READY AND WERE WAITING ON THE steps of Rose's house for our ride to the party. Nas and I were wearing cool suits Rose had found in her brother's closet. Her brother, who it turned out was Émile Bargeron! Only one of the best semipro skaters in the world! (He used his mother's maiden name instead of Bordage, which seemed like a missed opportunity, because what skater wouldn't want to be called Bordage—the word *board* was right there!) I was also carrying the messenger bag with the prophecy book. There was no way we were leaving anything behind after what had happened at the Catacombs.

"I look so fly," Nas said, admiring the rolled-up sleeves of his jacket, which showed the silk lining that was printed with palm trees and a sunset.

"Yeah, I still can't believe your brother is ÉMILE BARGERON!" I said to Rose. I was wearing one of Émile's longer jackets, in a deep green color, with shiny black elbow patches. It was the nicest thing I'd ever worn. I'd gone from knowing no one in Paris to putting on designer clothes for a fancy museum party. I thought I was immersing myself pretty well. Wait until Evan and Darren heard about this. "What's he like?"

"To you, he's this super-amazing skater with an attitude. But to me, he's an annoying big brother who burps in my face," Rose said. Then she smirked. "You know, the way people aren't the way you guess from the outside. Just like you thought I was a snobby rich girl but, really, I have problems like everyone else and wish my parents never split and my dad would stop acting like I'm incapable of breathing without a car waiting for me."

"Anyway, the waiting car came in handy," I said.

"But..." Rose gave us a look like she was expecting more.

"I'm sorry if we judged you," Nas said.

"It was totally Nas," I said. "I thought you were cool from the moment we met."

"And you both are more fun than a tunnel of dead bodies," Rose said. "And maybe even the party we're going to."

"What's that, kids?" A man in a tuxedo who I guessed had to be Rose's dad had stepped outside. His silver bow tie matched his hair. He held out a hand for me and Nas to shake.

"Monsieur Bordage, nice to meet you," Nas said. "I'm Nasim."

I followed Nas's lead. Mr. Bordage said, "Nasim, Owen, it's a pleasure to meet you." He gave our outfits a once-over. "You dress like my son."

I wasn't sure if he meant it as a compliment but I took it as one, so I said, "Thank you."

Madame LaForge emerged onto the steps behind Mr. Bordage. "Are we ready?" she said, just as a limousine pulled up to the front of the house. She waited for Mr. Bordage to help her down the stairs and they each got in the limo. Rose sighed and followed, gesturing for Nas and me to join her.

I wanted to check the limo for snacks but since I hoped to make a good impression, I didn't. And I barely had time to. The museum wasn't far from Rose's house.

"We're here," LaForge said. She pointed out the

window. We were slowing down in front of what must have been the Musée des Arts et Métiers. Not that I could see much of the building: The front was blocked by a giant, rainbow-striped hot-air balloon with a banner across it that said JULES VERNE: INVENTOR OF THE FUTURE.

"It looks perfect, doesn't it?" LaForge said dreamily as the driver, Martin, pulled to a stop in front of the museum's main entrance, where a purple carpet had been laid out. She looked at the bag on my lap. "You know, you can check that at the cloakroom inside," she said.

"It's part of Owen's look," Rose said, before I could say anything. We'd all agreed beforehand not to let the book or medallion out of our sight.

"Whatever Owen thinks," LaForge said. She gave a small wave and an air kiss to everyone in the car and stepped onto the walkway. "I must go check on how things are proceeding, but I'll see you at the party! I can't wait to hear what you all think of the exhibit. I'm very proud of it."

From inside the car, we all watched as LaForge made her VIP entrance. She stopped and talked to a few people, including two American actors who'd been in one of the new *Star Wars* movies. "She's so cool," Nas said to me.

"She is very cool," Mr. Bordage said admiringly. Rose rolled her eyes.

Martin drove to a second entry point and stopped. It was the non-VIP entrance but it was still flooded with well-dressed people chatting until they had to take their seats. We exited the car with Mr. Bordage. Rose stood up straighter in her gown, which was made of a lavender T-shirt with a poufy ballerina skirt decorated with golden ornaments shaped like mermaids and octopuses and divers. She seemed to fit right in with the crowd, even though we were the youngest people here. A lot of the guests looked like they could have been friends of Professor Bessier. The men were in suit coats that buttoned high on the waist with long tails dropping down, and some of the women had on long, full skirts. I counted three monocles and four sets of aviator goggles within the first ten seconds of getting out of the car.

A museum employee in an old-fashioned top hat escorted Mr. Bordage and the three of us to a row of seats right in front of the hot-air balloon.

We sat down and watched as other guests found their rows. I held the bag with the book in front of my feet, and patted the inside pocket of Émile's coat, where I'd stowed the medallion to make sure it was safe.

After more murmuring and shuffling as people got seated, a tall, broad-shouldered guy in a dark suit came to the podium and welcomed everyone. He said he was head of the museum's foundation but he looked like an action-movie star. He introduced Madame LaForge as the curator of the museum and organizer of the night's festivities. After some clapping, LaForge strode to the podium, smiling at everyone gathered. She flashed us an extra-large grin before she started her speech.

"If I could have a dinner party and invite anyone, living or dead, my guest of choice would be Jules Verne. I would love to ask him what he thinks of our present world, and what he predicts for our future, because that is what he did in all his work. He forecast the machines and innovations we'd enjoy long before they existed."

I turned around, sensing a small ripple of movement behind me. People were pointing at the sky, where a plane was spelling out the name of the exhibit from its tail.

"Ahh, you've all noticed our skywriter," LaForge went on. "Skywriting, for example, was something Verne predicted in his book *In the Year 2889*, while he also had the notion to create rockets from fireworks, in his book *From the Earth to the Moon*." She held a brass instrument with a curved handle and a pointed tip over her head and pressed a small lever on the handle. A burst of multicolored sparks streamed from the end, and a small rocket shot out and exploded into a massive flower of rainbow glimmers. LaForge admired the display as even larger fireworks started to go off in the sky behind the museum and a band near her played music that the program said was written for the 1902 film *A Trip to the Moon*, based on a Jules Verne story. "While I'd love to run down the entire list of Jules Verne's brilliant predictions, that would take me all night. So instead, I invite you to see firsthand more of the amazing devices that originated in his mind. Please, join me. The exhibit is open!" The big guy handed LaForge an enormous brass scissors, and she cut through a golden satin ribbon that was tied across the doors of the museum.

Guests watched as a few more fireworks shimmered across the sky, then when the final rocket burst in a purple, green, and blue shower of sparks and the music ended, they started to file in past LaForge, who greeted everyone like they were her favorite person ever. When we got to the door, LaForge clasped Rose's shoulder. "I'm so glad you all could come," she said. "I think you'll really find this interesting. And the food is delicious. I approved the menu myself."

Rose mumbled thanks but knelt down to play with a strap on her shoe, leaving LaForge's hand dangling in the air. LaForge caught me noticing this and gave a little shrug. I felt bad for her. Rose could be a little nicer on the lady's big night. Rose's dad took LaForge by the arm and escorted her inside the museum. LaForge said more hellos and hugged a woman in a jumpsuit that looked like she'd stolen it from an astronaut.

I whispered to Rose, "I get that it's weird to try to like this lady who's not your mom, but if your dad is dating her, you're lucky."

Rose watched as LaForge introduced Mr. Bordage to the spacesuit lady. "She's okay, I guess," she said. "She just...bugs me for some reason." Rose slipped away from us to take a mini quiche off a passing tray. Nas and I lagged behind, looking up at the high, sculpted ceilings of the museum. "I've never seen a museum like this," I said to him. "It looks like a church."

Nas had flipped his program to the back. "This says it was, once. It's an abbey, but it was converted to a museum by revolutionaries who wanted it to celebrate scientific achievement, sort of in a rebellious move against the church."

"Wow," I said, actually meaning it. I looked up and stared at an old flying machine suspended from the domed ceiling. I felt like I was in a movie. Rose was deeper in the crowd, with a bored expression as her dad introduced her to someone in a top hat. "Speaking of rebels, why do you think Rose is so anti-LaForge?"

Nas shrugged. "Maybe Rose thinks it's an act? Like,

150

LaForge and her dad are getting serious and LaForge is being nice to try and impress her."

Rose glanced back at him and Nas peered down at his feet, like he was worried she'd heard.

"Maybe," I said. "I think she's nice."

"It's easy for us to like LaForge because she's not dating our dad. Guess I shouldn't have acted like that. I mean, Rose may be rich, but she still has her own stuff to deal with," Nas said.

I was about to ask Nas if he'd had any wrong first impressions of me—besides that I had a weak stomach—when a waiter gave us each a small plate with a small sandwich shaped like a rocket ship on it.

Perfect. Food would keep me from asking uncomfortable questions. I bit into the little sandwich and realized it was the butteriest, most delicious grilled cheese I'd ever tasted. "LaForge wasn't lying about the food," I said to Nas. "What is this?"

"That's a croque monsieur, monsieur." The waiter had come up behind me and was extending a tray with more of the sandwiches on it. I put one, then two, then three on my plate and caught the server's expression, which silently said three was the limit.

But now that I knew French grilled cheese was superior to all others, I would have to tell my mom that as long as we were living in Paris, we could definitely do better than snail pizza.

Rose returned with two plates of chocolate éclairs and crackers with tiny orange bubbles on them. "Caviar or chocolate?"

"Both," I said. As I took one of each from her plate and transferred it to mine, I had the same weird sensation from the Catacombs that someone was behind me. I patted the pocket again, to check that the medallion was still there. I knew I should relax. This event had a ton of security. No ten-year-old or purple-coated weirdo was going to rob me here.

We ate and moved around the exhibit, trying to see past people to some of Jules Verne's innovations. The echoes of everyone's conversation made the air around us buzz with noise, and from the number of times I heard Jules Verne mentioned, these were all super fans. I felt bad for Bessier not getting to see this and got a little chill remembering the woman at the collège saying that foul play was suspected. I thought of Bessier getting into the car with the two men and how that stuff sometimes went down in movies. A shiver went through me and I felt a twitch in my shoulder blades, like someone was watching my back. Besides Bessier, no one had any reason to connect us to the book. That person at the Catacombs probably had just been a pickpocket.

An ancient elevator motor, a model of a high-speed train, a Taser, a small model of a submarine—almost as elaborate as Bessier's—and even a clunky old fax machine were all supposedly things Jules Verne had "invented" in his books. Yep, Bessier would have been in heaven here. So would my mom.

I was reading a plaque about how in one of his books, Jules Verne had talked about a spaceship manned by an animal crew, and how the first real-life space voyage was "manned" by a dog named Laika, when LaForge appeared on a platform in front of a cross-sectioned submarine.

"Now that you've had some time to marvel," she said, "I'd like to thank the Jules Verne Society for sponsoring our exhibit, and tonight's gala. As president of the society, I, along with our members, like Édouard Bordage"—she tilted her champagne glass toward Rose's dad—"am dedicated to preserving Jules Verne's legacy. It's not often dangerous work, but as many of you know, the vice president of our society, Charles Bessier, has disappeared. While I'm certain this has nothing to do with Jules Verne, Charles is a passionate member of our community, and I'd like to toast to his safe return."

LaForge lifted her glass, and the rest of the crowd did the same.

Rose nudged both Nas and me with her elbows. "I didn't know Bessier and LaForge knew each other. Isn't it weird that they're both in this society?"

I thought it was weirder that I'd just been thinking about Bessier and now LaForge had brought him up. But no. I didn't agree with Rose that it was strange she and Bessier were both members of this group. LaForge was probably a member of all kinds of societies, and she was a Jules Verne scholar, too. And Bessier...? I said to Rose, "Of course Bessier was a member of a Jules Verne society. Did you see his office? You don't have multiple toy *Nautiluses* for nothing."

"Maybe," Rose murmured. The toast ended with applause, and LaForge stepped away from the podium, pulling Rose's dad from his seat over to a screen printed with designs of some of the exhibit inventions. She posed alongside him as a photographer snapped several shots. Rose's dad laughed at something LaForge said, and Rose scowled.

"How about we look for more éclairs?" I suggested as a way to distract Rose and because I'd eaten the first one too fast and wanted to savor the next one.

"I'm not hungry," she said. "And I have a better idea."

CHAPTER TWENTY-FOUR

The VIP Tour

"THIS PARTY IS BORING," ROSE SAID. "BUT WE DON'T have to stay. Follow me."

Nas and I exchanged a look that was one part "This party isn't that boring. There are desserts everywhere!" and one part "But we better do what Rose says." She seemed irritated. I didn't know much about Rose's mom, or what happened when her parents split up, but it had to be hard to see your dad with a girlfriend. I had never even met my dad—my mom said she'd tell me about him when the time was right, but that hadn't happened yet.

Rose cut through a group of guests who barely

glanced at us. The good thing about everyone here thinking we were just some kids who'd been dragged along to the event was that no one was paying attention as we slipped along the back side of a large display devoted to Jules Verne's prediction of newscasts.

She headed for a freestanding metal staircase that zigzagged up from the center of the abbey floor and ended in a platform that gave you a better view of the old one-person plane hanging from the ceiling. But she passed that staircase and took us toward another twin set of marble stairs that connected to another level of the museum. She dashed up them two at a time, not even pausing to look at a flying machine that was even older than the one-person plane. It had canvas-covered wings and a teeny seat and looked incredibly unsafe. I thought it was pretty cool, but maybe Rose had seen it a thousand times.

Rose raced through an exhibit hall that contained cross-sections of old cars and through a door that was for employees.

"Should we be in here?" I asked, like I hadn't crossed police tape to get into Bessier's office.

Rose rolled her eyes. "It's just LaForge's office," she said, pointing to a frosted glass door. She pushed on it and it swung open. "We're only cutting through."

LaForge's office was very different from Bessier's.

It wasn't that it was empty or anything, but Bessier's office told you he loved Jules Verne, and LaForge's was much harder to read. On the wall were framed brochures of previous museum exhibitions, and one photo of LaForge with a guy in a suit. "That's the French president," Nas said, when he saw me studying it. She had one neat bookcase with a few art books and some other books with titles like *Discoveries of Man*.

Just beyond the offices was another door that Rose was waiting by. "Seriously, the only good thing about my dad dating a museum curator is getting to see the secret parts of this place." She waved for Nas and me to hurry.

"Is this off-limits, too?" I asked. Hadn't we done enough trespassing for one day?

Rose shrugged and pushed through the door. Did no one lock anything around here? "Not if you know where it is," she said, way cooler about this than me or Nas. "They call this section the Attic."

"Whoa," Nas and I said in hushed voices. The Attic might have been more interesting than the museum. Mostly because nothing was behind glass. An open crate contained piles of clock faces. Intricate models of Formula 1 race cars. Rows of boxy old TVs stacked on top of one another. An ancient-looking sundial. A wooden chest of watches and egg timers.

"If you can think of a machine, it's probably here," Rose said.

I picked up a pocket watch from the chest. It was still ticking and displayed the right time. Nas wandered up to an old buggy car with open sides and sat down behind the high steering wheel.

"What the…" I dropped the watch back into the chest and walked up to a silver person in a bowler hat and suit, like C-3PO's well-dressed cousin. I was about to reach out to touch it when it slapped my hand away. Not hard, and its arm made a creaky sound like it needed oil, but it was a definite slap.

"Hey!" I said, jumping back. "He slapped me."

"It's motion-activated," Rose said. "And a she. Thérèse, meet Nas and Owen."

Thérèse turned her head slowly toward us. "A pleasure to meet you, Nas and Owen."

"He's Nas," I said. "I'm Owen."

Thérèse had already gone back to staring straight ahead. "She's a pretty old automaton. She basically slaps and says it's nice to meet people, then goes to sleep."

"I had a great-aunt like that once," I said. "Her name was Millie."

Nas hopped out of the car and asked Rose, "Why isn't this stuff on display?"

She shrugged. "They phase out exhibits. Sometimes

they go to other museums, other times, they wind up here," Rose explained. She ducked behind the wall of TVs, and we could hear her rummaging around. "But I thought you should see this."

Rose emerged, holding a black box and two hand-sized paddles. "Meet the XBox's great-great-great-great-grandfather." She unraveled a cord and went back behind the TVs. One of the screens made a staticky hiss and came to life. There was a white rectangle on a black background, divided down the center with a dotted line. On either side were small white bars. Rose pressed a button and a white square materialized. She tossed me one of the paddles and the square started to move toward my bar.

"What am I supposed to do?"

"You hit the ball before it touches the wall behind you."

"Ball? Wall? It's a square and a line! What do you mean?"

"That I just scored a point," Rose said. She passed her controller to Nas. "Here, you try. I play winner."

"Isn't this game like fifty years old?" Nas said. "I still don't get why it's in a museum, though."

Rose grinned. "It's an invention, just like every video game. We have every system and every game you can think of."

160

Normally, hearing that would have made me demand to see all the games right away, but I was already way too into Pong. It was so simple but addictive. Pure competition. And a really nice way to not think about whether a person had been following us downstairs.

We played for I didn't even know how long, and it wasn't until several of the watches started beeping and clanging as their alarms went off that I said, "Whoa, how long have we been in here?" I said.

"I guess about an hour," Nas said. "We should go back to the party."

Rose sighed. "You're right," she said. "Come on, there's a staircase through that door."

We followed Rose out of the Attic and down a set of narrow steps that spat us out into a darkened exhibit hall, with cases filled with automatons. Most of them were human ones, like Thérèse, but there was one that had tiger fur and could swivel its head and raise its paw. None of them could slap me, though. They were all behind glass but the glow of their faces in the dim light filtering through a high window above us was a little spooky. Then we heard voices.

At the far end of the room, a few people from the party pulled back a dark-blue curtain and stepped inside. There was a scraping sound, followed by muffled voices and a door opening and closing.

"What do you think that's about?" I said.

"I'm not sure," Rose said. We stood as still as we could next to the case of automatons as three more people turned into the exhibit hall. Moonlight fell on a gold lapel pin one of the men wore, and even in the dark, I could make out the shape of a nautilus shell, just like on the medallion.

"Do you think we should check it out?" Even if their pins matched the medallion, it didn't really mean anything. The nautilus shell was part of Jules Verne's brand, it seemed, and the medallion we'd found had clearly been in the Catacombs for a long time.

"Yeah, let's go," Rose said, leading the way.

"Okay, guess we're doing this," I said to Nas.

"Maybe I'll remember today as the first time I got invited to a fancy party and the first time I got kicked out of a fancy party," Nas said.

Rose slipped behind the curtain and we were a few steps behind her. As the fabric swung back into place with a small whoosh, I looked around. We were in a small alcove, facing a solid wood door, with a golden mega-sized version of our medallion hanging at the top of it. All right, maybe the shell was a common Jules Verne symbol, but this seemed like more than a coincidence.

I pushed on the door, and it didn't budge. Then,

beneath the medallion, a narrow sideways door about the size of a mail slot slid open and a set of bulging eyeballs behind a pair of giant goggles peered out at us. "Please stay with the party. This area is off-limits." The voice was deep and threatening. The small door shut.

"Okay, guys, guess we should get back," I said. I'd already been kicked out of Bessier's seminar. I didn't need to disappoint Mom more by getting involved in some weird Jules Verne crime syndicate. Except…

I knocked on the door within a door again.

A hand pulled the door open, but only about an inch. "I said, please go."

"Hold on," I said. "I have this." I produced the medallion from inside the coat. I could get my mom to believe that mingling with a Jules Verne crime syndicate was good for my education. Plus, we'd gone through so much trouble to get the medallion, we might as well use it.

The small door slid open all the way as I dangled the chain in front of the blinking set of eyeballs.

"Why didn't you say so?" The panel slid shut and the door swung inward. Standing behind the door was a youngish guy in a brown suit wearing steampunk goggles that magnified his eyes. "Do join the member-ship," he said in a voice that was still deep but much more welcoming than before. He gestured to the room behind him.

Where the museum was lots of stone and sculpture, like a lot of the churches in Paris, this room was like someone's idea of the future—if that someone lived about a hundred years ago. The walls were made of pressed bronze panels held together with oversized bolts. They gave the room the feeling of being part of a larger machine or an engine. A darker bronze bar ran along one wall, surrounded by small groupings of plush blue chairs set around tables that looked like oversized bolts. At several of those, society members talked and drank from brass mugs. Most of them were wrapped up in their conversations, though a few glanced up and shot us curious looks.

"What is this place?" Nas whispered as a waitress in an undersea diving helmet brought a tray of drinks to a table.

"I don't know," Rose said. "LaForge definitely never showed me this room."

At the opposite end of the space, a man in a tuxedo was pointing at the ceiling, and the woman he was with craned her neck back. I followed her gaze upward and gasped. "Whoa," I said. The high ceiling had been painted to look like a sprawling aerial view of Paris, so that if you were standing on the floor, it seemed as if you were in the sky, looking down at the city. I found Le Dôme and the collège and even the general area where my apartment with Mom was.

"I live over here," Nas said, pointing at an area across the Seine and northeast of the collège.

"One of my brother's close friends lives there," Rose said. Her gaze landed somewhere over my shoulder, and she subtly nodded so we'd look. "What's going on over there?" Across the room, a cluster of society people were gathered around another display.

"Let's go see," I said. We inched closer. As we neared the center of the room, the floor began to vibrate and the walls thrummed as a low rumble rolled over the room.

"Whoa," I said, planting my feet as my legs shook with the ground. Nas grabbed the top of a chair to steady himself. "Is it an earthquake?"

"I wouldn't think so," Rose said calmly, even though she'd balled her hands into fists. "Whatever it is, these people must be used to it."

She was right. No one else seemed panicked—they just clutched their drinks more tightly like the room rattling was an everyday thing—and the vibration died down.

We got as close as we could to the center of the room, trying to see whatever was behind the velvet ropes and

166

attracting a crowd. Two guys in top hats stepped right in front of us, blocking our view. I crouched down to shove my face in the gap between them, squinting to see what they were admiring.

"What is that thing?" Nas said, also making use of the gap. "Some kind of really fancy garbage disposal?"

The society members were gathered around a metal box, about three feet tall, and decorated with brass renderings of hot-air balloons, submarines, and rocket ships. I slowly read the words on a plaque. "See the world through"—a woman walked in front of me—"my eyes."

Top Hat Guy Number One said, "Bizarre contraption. If we're even sure it's a contraption. It doesn't seem to do anything."

The other man was snapping a picture. "Have some imagination, Guillaume. The society must dedicate resources to solve this mystery."

A mystery. Hmmm.

Someone stepped up behind us, and a hand closed over my shoulder. A giant hand. "Kid, what are you doing in here?" I spun around and came face-to-face with a massive security guard with hair past his shoulders. He looked like Aquaman on land.

I flashed the medallion and said, "He let us in," pointing to the stool near the door. But the guy in the goggles was gone. The security guard raised one eyebrow. "Not a necklace," he said. "I'm instructed only to grant admission to this gathering with a pin. Where's yours?"

I opened my mouth but couldn't think of anything funny to say. Or anything to say at all. I started to back away.

He grabbed my wrist. Tight. "Again, where's your pin?" Then he scowled at Rose and Nas. "And theirs."

"You're not our teacher," Rose said, loud enough for the whole room to hear. "You should stop touching my friend. We'll go tell our chaperone."

The security guard loosened his grip on my arm and swiveled his head to search for our imaginary chaperone. He spoke into a device on his wrist and turned back toward me. "Where'd you get that?" He pointed at the medallion, which I was now wearing around my neck.

"It was my grandma's...," I said. The security guy raised the hand that wasn't grabbing my arm to signal for someone to come over. My heart pounded.

"Hey," I said. "There's our chaperone!" I pretended to wave at someone across the room. The guard dropped my arm and I started to run, with Rose and Nas right behind me.

"Give me that necklace! That's not yours! The society will want to see it!"

People turned to watch as we dodged a waitress carrying a tray of drinks that each let off its own steam. A man in a bowler hat lifted his cane as if to block us and I hurdled over it, kicking it out of his hands as I did. Rose and Nas circled around the guy on his other side.

We headed the way we had come in, and the guy who'd let us in was standing in front of us with his arms folded over his chest. "What's going on? What do you have?"

"You don't wanna know," I said, clutching my stomach like I might barf.

The steampunk guy turned a little green and sidestepped away from us, leaving the secret door easy to get to. We pushed through and fell out of the room through the dark blue curtain. Then we raced back through the automaton room and down a corridor that led to an exit door at the rear of the museum.

We bolted outside and stood with our backs against the stone wall of the museum, catching our breath. "Well, they were kind of uptight," I said.

"Yeah, for sure," Nas said. He peered around the corner of the building toward the entrance. He turned back to Rose and me. "Should we go back inside? Find your dad so we don't lose our ride home?"

We were watching the caterers load up their truck.

A shadow fell on the path in front of us and Officer

Sadface from Bessier's office was standing with his hands on his hips. "Enjoy the party?" he said, pulling his tie looser.

"Until you showed up, yes," Rose said. Nas and I laughed a little.

"Very funny," Sadface said, looking a little flustered. "I have some questions for you three."

Great. An interrogation. I would have been better off at the apartment, with or without Mom.

"And my family has a lawyer," Rose said. Nas and I shot each other a look, not believing Rose had really said that.

But the cop glared at her. "Your teacher, Professor Bessier, was he acting strange the last day you saw him?"

Yes, I thought. Instead, I said, "He was obsessed with Jules Verne. He was strange every day." Behind me, Rose and Nas murmured their agreement.

"Look, I don't have time for sarcasm; it's very important you answer me," he said. He pointed at his car—not a regular cop car, but a dingy beige sedan— parked at the curb. "Or I could bring you in for questioning." He flashed his badge.

But we were saved when the shiny Rolls rolled up to a stop next to the cop's ugly car.

Rose's dad leaped out of the back seat, followed by LaForge. "What can I do for you, Officer?" he said. He spoke calmly, but not like he was actually calm. More like he was a guy in a movie who was holding it together just enough to keep his anger from getting out of control. "This is a private event. I'm sure your superiors wouldn't like to hear from myself and Chantal LaForge that you came and disrupted it to hound a few kids."

The cop's face grew red, but he didn't apologize. "I will use more official channels next time." He scowled as he stomped back to his car, and I wondered what he meant by "official channels."

CHAPTER TWENTY-FIVE

Impromptu Sleepover

"You don't always have to swoop in like that, Dad," Rose was saying as we all got back into the car. "I can take care of myself."

Her dad yanked his tie loose and stared at her. "You're my only daughter, and believe it or not, you don't yet know everything, or what can happen when you walk around thinking you do. Now, why was that officer asking you questions?"

Rose shrugged. She shot LaForge a look. "He's looking for your friend, Professor Bessier." If LaForge found this strange, she didn't show it.

"It's upsetting that he's gone missing. He's such an

intelligent man," LaForge said with concern. "But I would hope the officer should know better than to drag three innocent students into it."

Were we innocent, though? I thought about the book in the messenger bag near my feet.

"Exactly," Rose's dad said, more gently this time. "The officer has no right to lurk around talking to you and your friends. If I don't protect you, who will?"

Rose kicked the leather seat. "I don't need to be protected," she said. "Why don't you worry about your own life?" She shot a glance at LaForge when she said this. Like LaForge was what her dad needed to worry about. Talk about awkward. Especially after LaForge had taken our side.

But LaForge didn't flinch. "It was an eventful night," she said. "And I'm sure the police encounter has you both wound up." Now she placed a hand on Rose's dad's arm, like it was something she did every day. Rose's eyes flashed on LaForge's hand but she turned and stared out the window as LaForge continued talking. "Maybe you should all come back to our place and I can fix you something else to eat. I can make sandwiches." She looked right at me and Nas, like she could hear my stomach growling. The party food was good, but it had all been in miniature.

"Actually, we can't go back to *our* place. We're

invited to sleep over at Owen's. His mom already put together a fancy meal for us....She's been...baking, and preparing, all day....We can't not show up," Rose said, before I could tell her that my mom didn't really do fancy. And might not even show up. She leaned forward in her seat toward Martin. "Martin, you can let us out here, it's a short walk. D'accord, Papa?" Rose glared at LaForge's hand on her dad's arm and then right into her dad's sheepish face.

"Of course," he said. "Tell your mother thank you, Owen. And Rose, we'll discuss your behavior later."

Martin had pulled off to the curb in a neighborhood that I was pretty sure was nowhere near our apartment. But Rose was so intense, I would have been scared to argue with her.

After we'd hopped out of the car, Rose walked ahead of us. Nas and I trudged behind her. "She's really angry," Nas said. "You'd think she'd be glad her dad scared the cop away."

"Yeah, plus, I don't know what she thinks I have to eat at my apartment. There's some snail pizza left, but that's it." Maybe I could change that if Mom was actually home. She'd promised me a fun weekend, and it was Friday night. I fished out my cell phone and dialed my mom. It rang and rang.

Usually my mom would send a text while the phone

rang with my number, to let me know she couldn't talk and to make sure I was okay. Not this time.

I had a little flash of worry—why wasn't she answering—but that quickly turned to anger. She was probably at a party or a lecture with other scientists and I wasn't important enough to pick up the phone for.

When her voice mail came on, I almost said something hurtful.

But Nas was watching me dial, and I didn't want to get into my whole story. So, I pretended like everything was fine.

"Hey, Mom, it's O. I was hoping to bring some friends over for you to meet. I thought we could have dinner and a sleepover. I guess you're at the lab. It's no big deal, just checking to see if you were around. Love you. Bye."

Rose finally rejoined us. "I'm sorry, Owen, I didn't mean for you to bother your mom. Do you think we could sleep over anyway?"

I was about to explain the snail pizza situation when Nas chimed in. "Come to my house. My mom will love to feed you guys."

CHAPTER TWENTY-SIX

Somehow, I Eat Even More

Friday, June 19, 8:30 p.m.

WE TOOK TWO MÉTRO TRAINS TO NAS'S NEIGHBOR-hood, getting off just outside the Père-Lachaise Cemetery. Rose told me that a lot of famous people were buried there but, after the Catacombs, I felt like I had had my fill of the dead for a while.

We walked a few blocks past storefronts with signs I couldn't read—not because my French was bad, but because they were in other languages. The apartment buildings here were less ornate than near the collège, and a group of kids ran on the sidewalk out in front of them, weaving circles around streetlamps as they played tag.

"I'm on the third floor," Nas said, turning into the narrow stairwell of a blue building. As soon as we set foot on the first step, a woman's voice called down from above. "Nasim, is that you? Why haven't you called?"

"I texted, Mom. I told you, we got to go to a museum. Extra credit," Nas yelled up the stairs. "And I'm safe. I brought guests." He whispered to us, "She loves guests."

Nas's mom met us on the landing. She was shorter than Nas but seemed stronger by the way she dragged him into the apartment. She beamed at us as she did it, though. "It's so nice to have Nasim's friends come over!" she said. Her eyes crinkled at the corners. I liked her right away.

A man I guessed was Nas's dad was in the doorway. "Look at you," he said to Nasim. "All dressed up. No hoodie. We should take a photo to commemorate the occasion." He nodded and smiled at Rose and me. "Who are your friends?"

When Nas introduced us, his dad stepped away from the door. "Oh, Owen and Rose, the scholars you told us about. Welcome!"

"Yes, come in, come in!" his mom said, only letting

his arm go once we'd passed through the door, like she wanted to make sure he didn't leave again.

Nas's apartment wasn't much bigger than the one Mom and I were in. The front door led straight to a living room and dining area, just like at our place. A boy and two girls who I guessed were Nas's younger siblings made faces at Nas, and one of the girls, the younger one, said, "You look weird," when she saw his clothes. To Rose, she said, "That dress is so pretty."

"Thank you," Rose said. "I like your sneakers." Nas's sister's Vans were covered in drawings and patterns she must have done herself.

"Kids, say hello to Rose and Owen, Nasim's new friends from his Jules Verne seminar," Nas's dad said, holding his arms out wide.

His family greeted us.

"I hope you're hungry!" Nas's mom said, now taking Rose and me by the hand. "Here." Nas's mom took two plates from the top of a stack on the dining table, where platters of food were laid out. She handed the plates to us, then started loading food onto them as she told us what each dish was.

There was tajine, a stew made with lamb and onions that smelled amazing, and an egg dish called shakshuka. "And this is my ditalini with my tomato sauce," Nas's mom said.

"Ditalini. Isn't that Italian?" I asked. I loved Italian food.

"Libya was under Italian rule during some of its formative years," Nas's father said as he snuck behind us to take a heaping spoonful of Nas's mom's pasta. "Your sauce is so good, Khadija." Nas's mom beamed. "Better than my sister's."

"They're friendly competitors," Nas's dad said to us. "Or, most of the time friendly."

After we'd eaten two plates of food, Nas's mom took the dishes away and told his dad and little brother that they were on washing duty. Then she set out two trays—one filled with different cookies and bars, and another crowded with fancy-looking chocolate balls and squares.

"Nas's aunt made the abambar, these little almond cookies, and her husband made the basbousa—this cake—from his mother's recipe. And the other sweets are from Nasim's cousin Amna. She's studying to be a chocolatier," Nas's mom said. She proudly showed us the tray of sweets. "They dropped by earlier. I wish you could have met them."

Nas's littler sister skipped up to take a treat off the plate. "Amna made almond truffles, and she said this other one is a dark chocolate with a cherry thread through it," she said. Then she jutted out her chin and said, almost like a threat, "And if you don't like sweets, I don't know if you can be trusted."

"No problem there," Nas said. "Owen probably couldn't be trusted alone with a bunch of candy."

I wasn't able to respond because I was already trying the dark-chocolate-cherry thing. Between LaForge's cocoa and the éclair and now the desserts, I'd almost forgotten about my stolen Starbursts. Though I did like to have one right before bed, and it stung that I wouldn't get to for the second night in a row.

Rose took two truffles and a square of basbousa. "Nas, you're so lucky," she said. "Your mom is a terrific cook. Do you cook, too, or just DJ?"

"Shh," Nas said. He checked to see if anyone else had heard. "DJing is supposed to just be a hobby for me for now. They don't want me doing it outside the house until I'm older."

Nas's mom appeared at his shoulder. "Are your friends staying over?"

"If that's okay," Nas said.

"Of course," Nas's mom told us. "Nasim's class-mates are always welcome."

We helped put away the dishes and pushed some of the chairs to the corners of the room. Nas's mom handed Rose and me each a stack of blankets, sheets, and pil-lows. "Get some rest," she said to us, and squeezed Nas in a tight hug that seemed to embarrass him, but that made me miss my own mom. "I don't want your parents thinking I didn't take responsible care of you."

I texted my mom to tell her I was staying at Nas's, almost hoping she'd say I needed to come home. Or at least that she was disappointed we wouldn't be spending a fun French Friday together.

When a few minutes passed by with no response, I thought to myself that she'd better be at a great party to ignore me for this long.

CHAPTER TWENTY-SEVEN

Jules's Diary

NAS'S ROOM WAS MUCH SMALLER THAN ROSE'S AND HAD no signs of his personality. Or at least the personality we'd gotten to know. He had one overflowing bookshelf and a few posters—the periodic table, the solar system, and heroes of literature with lines from Shakespeare, Jane Austen, Langston Hughes, and my old favorite guy, Charles Dickens.

"So where do you keep your DJ stuff?" I asked, trying to figure it out.

Nas opened a trunk at the foot of his bed that appeared to be filled with textbooks. But he moved a math and a history book from the top and revealed a secret panel that he lifted. Underneath were two crates of records and his portable turntables.

"Wow," I said. "You and Bessier should get together and talk about building secret compartments."

Rose was looking at a family photo in a frame on Nas's desk.

"I like your family," Rose said. "It must be nice to have your sisters and brother."

I shared a smile with her. At least I wasn't the only one who felt that way.

"Sure, if you like people poking their nose in everything you do and sharing a bathroom with your siblings," Nas said.

"I never get to see my brother, he's so busy traveling," Rose said. She spread her sheet out on the floor and set down the pillow, then smoothed her blanket. "Hey, what do you guys think we should do tomorrow? Does the book say anything about the medallion?"

I pulled it out of the messenger bag's pouch. There were a few pages of drawings—or, doodles, really, mostly geometric shapes and cones and spheres—after the runic writing that had led us to the medallion.

"I don't know what this is," I said.

183

"We're not supposed to skip ahead, though," Nas reminded me.

"Just a peek?" I flipped forward and found a page of cursive writing. It looked like a diary entry and the handwriting was probably Jules Verne's, if we were going to believe he'd written this book. Which I did. If I'd had any doubts before, they'd been taken care of by going down into the Catacombs and pulling a necklace off a corpse. Jules Verne would have come up with that hunt.

The date at the top of the page was March 5, 1905. I'd memorized Jules Verne's birth, February 8, 1828, and death, March 24, 1905, in case of a test. So he'd written it not long before he died. That gave me the slightest chill. It said:

> Sometimes, I can't believe that my treasure is real. I've spent a lifetime amassing all that I needed—*more* than I needed—to have my most fanciful notions realized. But now that I'm faced with the end of my life, I can't simply let my treasure—my life's work— go to minds that would dishonor it. But I can safely state that, just as I dreamt, this fortune of mine is deeper than its beauty. When

accessed, it is greater than the sum of its parts;
it has potential to lead its owner to more
treasures and untold wonders, so long as they
know how to invest it. I have taken pains to
keep it safe, and in doing so, have found the
piece that makes the point. I only hope that
whoever goes to claim it will see how the whole
picture comes together.

"Is my French just bad or does that not make any sense?" I said.

"It's cryptic, for sure, but also it sounds like he buried a huge treasure. That if we invest will make us even richer?" Nas said. "Maybe this is some weird Bitcoin scam."

"Very funny," Rose said. She reread the page over my shoulder and pointed at the last line. "It has to be some kind of a riddle. But if there's a piece that makes the point, I don't know if we have that."

"Maybe we hit a dead end," I said. Rose was reaching for the book, so I handed it to her. Even though discovering a treasure would be great—part of me still wanted to go to Disney World to make up for the trip that had gotten canceled, and my mom's old Volvo was a wreck; treasure would fix that—I hated the idea of trying to piece together clues and not finding anything. "I bet this book is worth something. We could see what Madame LaForge says about it."

"That's a good idea," Nas said.

Rose shot us both a death glare. "Not so fast," she said.

CHAPTER TWENTY-EIGHT

Follow the Code to the Letter

Rose held up the page she had turned to.

"Oh great, another page that makes no sense," Nas said.

It was a series of letters in a circle, in no order that was even pronounceable.

Rose rolled her eyes. "It's obviously a code of some sort. He sent us to the Catacombs to take a necklace off a dead guy. You can't think he's just going to follow that up with, 'BTW, now I'll tell you exactly what to do.'"

"Well, no," I said with a sigh. "But that would be a lot easier. He could at least leave a clue to where to find the answer key for his code."

"If I'm going in order like the note said, then it's on the next page," Rose quipped. She was pacing around Nas's room as she carried the open book. She turned a page.

"Ha, I think this is something!" Rose said. I was already tired, but then again, Rose drank strong French coffee, so maybe she never slept. I also thought that maybe she seemed happier since we'd left the party and gotten to Nas's house. She seemed more at home in Nas's tiny room than her giant one.

"Look! This must be related to the letters on the last page. We just need to crack the code," Rose said. "There's probably a clue here."

Nas shook his head in disappointment. "But it's no good having letters with no corresponding value. Dead end," he said.

"We should sleep on it." Maybe it was the combination of ditalini, chocolate éclairs, and all the caviar and cheese, but I couldn't think clearly anymore. I felt worse than I had from the jet lag, like my eyeballs were made of lead and wanted to pull my head down to sleep. I spread the blanket Nas's mom had given me out on the floor and flopped back onto the pillow. As I lay down, the medallion slid backward from my chest, coming to a rest alongside my neck. I sat up to take it off. Holding it in my palm, I ran a finger over the nautilus shell emblem on the front, then turned it over. I hadn't paid much attention to the back of the pendant because it appeared smooth from a few feet away. But as I inspected it, I saw that tiny letters were engraved on the outer edge of the medallion's back side.

I sat up with a jolt. "The circle! It fits the circle!" I almost shouted.

"What are you talking about, Owen?" Rose said. "I think you do need sleep." I was too excited now. I felt like I'd had ten cups of French coffee without the stomachache. I leaned over Rose and set the medallion down in the middle of the circle of letters. There was an arrow pointing down at the top of the circle in the book, and another arrow pointing up on the medallion. When I lined them up, each letter in the book aligned with a corresponding letter on the necklace.

"It's a cipher!" Rose said.

"A what?" I asked.

"A cipher," Nas answered. "Like an old-school algorithm. Or a code, where each symbol represents something more recognizable. Like, how here every time we see a *Y* on the page, it's actually an *E*."

To make it easier, we wrote out the letters in the book and which letter they corresponded to on the medallion. We used the key we'd created to decode the short message on the next page. It didn't take very long.

"Give me your tired, your poor, your huddled masses yearning to breathe free. Vive la différence.... Let light lead the way!"

"That sounds familiar," I said. "Like historic."

But then again, the whole book was historic. And the message didn't tell us anything. I'd been expecting directions, like, "Go to the coffeeshop on the Rue Saint-Jacques and pull out the fifth brick in the third row" or something. This sounded like part of a poem, and I really never understood poetry.

But now Nas smacked me on the back. "No way. You got something, O." He went to his dresser and took down a photo taped to the wall. It was of a group of people standing in front of the Statue of Liberty. "This is my mom's sister and her family. They live in Queens," he said.

I stared at the photo. "Okay," I said. "But I don't get it."

"It's from an inscription on the Statue of Liberty," Nas said. "A poem."

I knew it was a poem. "But what does this poem have to do with anything?"

"I don't know. I just think this means the clue has something to do with the statue."

"So, we have to go to New York?" I said. "Can we do that *after* I get some sleep? I should probably tell my mom, too."

"Ha, I would love to go to New York just to try the pizza, but I don't think that makes sense," Rose said, shaking her head. "If Jules Verne did all this in 1905 and

191

right before he died, I don't think he made a journey to New York to hide a clue."

Rose had a point. Plus, there was the other nagging question. "What would the Statue of Liberty or this poem have to do with Jules Verne anyway?" I said.

Now Rose sprang to action, typing on her phone. "Well, this says the author, Emma Lazarus, was Verne's contemporary. She wrote the poem in 1883. Plus, I remember that the Statue of Liberty is mentioned in *Robur the Conqueror*, another Jules Verne book. Strange lights appear over the statue and then black flags with gold suns show up."

"Why are you in a Jules Verne seminar when you already know more about Jules Verne than anyone I know?" I asked her.

"To get out of the house." Rose smirked. Then her face got more serious. "Plus, the one thing that I can say about my dad is that he actually reads all the books he collects. And he read my brother and me a lot of Jules Verne."

Nas was searching something on his laptop. "That book you mentioned was published in 1886, a few years after the poem."

I shrugged. "I guess it's just that the first clue took us right to the Catacombs. And this feels like we should go to where the poem is."

Nas read more of the article on his screen. "I mean, in that book, *Robur the Conqueror*, the lights and flags also appear over the Eiffel Tower. Or is there somewhere with a sun symbol, like the black flags? Maybe we have to find that."

"I think it's simpler than that. Maybe we have to go to the *other* Statue of Liberty," Rose said.

"Oh, yeah," Nas said. He was nodding. "That makes sense."

"What do you even mean, the *other* Statue of Liberty?"

She let out an annoyed breath. "You're so American sometimes, Owen," she said. "The Statue of Liberty France gave to America is the biggest one, but it's not the only one. The sculptor made others, and they're all over the world. There are several in France."

"Great. So, how do we know which one to go to?" I asked.

Rose and Nas exchanged a look, as if French kids had taken a class on where all the extra Statues of Liberty were. "Well, there's the one in the Luxembourg Gardens, and there's another one on the Île aux Cygnes," Nas said.

"And one at the Musée des Arts et Métiers," Rose said while giving me an eye roll.

"Oh yeah," I said. Now I remembered passing by

193

a small version of the New York Statue of Liberty earlier that night. I'd been so busy trying to sample all the food, I hadn't given it much thought.

"Let's save that one for last. I don't feel like going back there," Rose said.

"Let's start with the one in the Luxembourg Gardens," Nas said.

I still wasn't entirely convinced that we'd interpreted the clue correctly, but I couldn't think of any alternatives. "Okay, I guess we know where to start our day tomorrow."

CHAPTER TWENTY-NINE

Saturday in the Garden

Saturday, June 20, 9:12 a.m.

THE NEXT MORNING, NAS'S MOM WOULDN'T LET US
leave the house until we'd all eaten a big breakfast. We
had to tell her and Nas's dad that we were headed to the
Luxembourg Gardens for a project on our next reading
assignment. I felt guilty making up a cover story and
even worse when she sent us out the door with home-
made lunches.

On the train, I zoned out, wondering if there'd really
even be anything hidden in the statue. Why had Jules
Verne taken so much trouble to hide this stuff? When

would we figure out what it all meant? And if we did, would a treasure Jules Verne had hidden more than one hundred years ago even be something that still seemed like a treasure? Like, I could hide a LeBron James rookie card today and maybe a hundred years or so from now, it would mean nothing to the person who found it. No, who was I kidding? That would be an awesome find in the 2120s.

"Owen," Nas said, shaking me away from the train window. "We're here, dude. Wake up."

"I wasn't sleeping," I said. *Just hoping we don't do all this work and end up finding a late-1800s version of a toaster oven.*

We came up from the Métro stop onto the street with a tour group. A lot of them headed into an enormous castle. "What's that building?" I asked.

"That's the Palais du Luxembourg," Nas said. "The upper houses of the French legislature work there but not on Saturdays. Yet it's still a tourist attraction."

"We're going to the gardens that surround it," Rose added.

"But there's no big fence or anything?" I was thinking of the White House and how the building was set way back by a bunch of grass that wasn't for walking around in. "Anyone can just hang out in the park?"

"Yeah," Rose said. "Isn't it great?"

I followed them as they cut through a stand of trees to the left of the castle. "We'll show you the fountain, too, while we're here," Rose said. "It's one of my favorite places."

"Mine too," Nas said. "But the queen who built it, Marie de Médicis, was kind of whack."

"She had an awful childhood and people manipulated her for her money," Rose said. She looked at me. "France disliked her because she was not from here and did favors for her Italian contacts. But she did build this beautiful fountain."

"Whoa," I said, as we turned into a clearing and the fountain came into view. Underneath an overhanging of willow trees was a huge pool with a stone monument at one end. A sculpture on top showed a big guy peering down at a couple who seemed to be kissing. When Rose had said "fountain," I'd thought of the one in the mall back home, a small square pool with a spout in the center. This was a thousand times more impressive, especially with the way the trees framed it. The fountain at the mall was right next to a kiosk selling hair straighteners.

What I noticed most was how quiet it was in this part of the park. Besides the three of us, there were just two older people, leaning against the stone railing around the shallow pool to look at a pair of ducks swimming in it.

I patted the medallion around my neck. Without Jules Verne and his treasure hunt, I might never have seen this special place.

"What do you like about this fountain more than others?" I asked Rose.

"It was my mother's favorite," she said. "She'd take me to the carousel and then walk me home by passing through here."

"Oh," I said. "You must miss her a lot."

"My mom is still alive. She just lives in Belgium most of the year," Rose said. "I'll probably go see her at the end of the summer. Is it just you and your mom?"

"I know my dad but they were never married," I said. "They're friends, but I don't see him that much."

"It sounds complicated," Rose said. I nodded but the truth was, I preferred having a dad that I treated like a distant uncle instead of having to go back and forth between two houses and families like some of my friends.

We made our way through another clump of trees and stepped out into the sun. We were behind the big castle building. Or in front of it? I wasn't sure. Here, there was a big pond where people sailed tiny boats, and on the grass that was mowed in neat circles, some people sunbathed on towels or ate sandwiches while seated on blankets and benches. The gardens were perfectly manicured with flowers in neat configurations, and the bushes around them trimmed at sharp angles. Statues dotted different spots in the park but they didn't seem to be in any particular order. And there was no dress code—some of the statues were dressed in military uniforms or royal clothes and others had on nothing at all.

Nas said he knew where the Statue of Liberty was, so Rose and I let him take the lead.

"Here it is," Nas finally said, stopping a few feet ahead of me and Rose. He was standing under a tree, looking up at the statue.

"Wait, what?" I said. I'd been expecting the statue to be looming over us, but it was only about ten feet tall and tucked under a tree. "Is this the whole statue?"

"Very funny," Rose said. "This was just a model for the bigger version."

I handed Rose my phone. "Can you take my picture? Like go way back, and then I'm going to stand with my hand out so it looks like I'm holding the statue."

Rose smiled at me.

"O, you're such a tourist," Nas said.

"Tourists gotta tour," I said. I turned my head and made a face like I didn't know how a giant statue had gotten into my hand. "How's it looking, Rose?"

"Hold on, and move a few inches to the left," Rose said as she knelt down to get the angle I wanted. Nas wandered away and began to read a placard next to the statue.

"Rose? O? I don't think this is going to work," he said.

"Are you kidding?" I said. I was pointing with my left hand at the Statue of Liberty that seemed to be in the palm of my right hand. Then, to Rose I added, "Nas isn't in the shot, right?"

"I mean, this statue isn't going to work," Nas said.

He was pointing at the placard. Rose and I went to see what it said. Of course, I was still struggling to read it when Rose said, "This is a replica!"

"I thought we already knew that," I said.

"No, this is a replica of that model," Nas said. "They made it much later because the original was being vandalized. So they moved that statue to the Musée d'Orsay in 2012."

"Okay, so do we go there?" I said.

"Let's stick to the plan and make the one on Île aux Cygnes our second stop," Nas said. "It's closer, anyway."

CHAPTER THIRTY

Brunch in the Sky

THE STATUE OF LIBERTY THAT WAS ON ÎLE AUX CYGNES was put there in 1889, according to the search I did on the walk to the Métro.

The Île aux Cygnes was a long, narrow island in the middle of the Seine. We'd gotten off the train near the Rouelle bridge and were headed toward the Grenelle bridge. The statue stood just past it. Instead of facing us, she looked out over the Seine. According to the internet, this statue faced toward the larger statue in the United States.

Bikers and joggers passed us in either direction on

the shady paths. In the Seine, a huge barge carrying piles of grain floated by. Smaller boats drifted past on either side. Another long, flat boat was stopped next to a dock that led off the island. A line of people were waiting to board. The boat's top deck had rows and rows of chairs. "That's a bateau-mouche. Another tourist thing but the views are pretty," Rose said. She pointed to a bateau-mouche passing by on the other side of us. People stood at the railings, snapping pictures of the Statue of Liberty's regal face.

We'd just come to the end of the island, and the back of the statue, which faced the water.

This one was bigger. By a lot. It was still nowhere near as tall as the one in New York City, or as wide, but it was on a platform, so it loomed at least seventy feet above us. I'd seen the Statue of Liberty with my mom when she'd presented at a conference at NYU.

Rose frowned as she stared at the statue. "The clue said, 'Let light lead the way.'"

"There are lightbulbs on the pedestal around her," Nas said.

Rose shook her head. "Those were added later. Jules Verne would have been dead by then."

"Maybe there's something with the angle of the sun," I suggested.

Rose didn't answer me. She was looking up at the statue with a determined expression. "He had to mean the torch," Rose said to no one in particular.

She was already walking toward the statue. Nas and I followed her as she raced ahead. "She's not thinking of climbing it, is she?" Nas said.

"There's no way," I said. "How would she even do that?"

We caught up to Rose at the front of the statue. Scaffolding led all the way up to the top. There were buckets and rags on the ground by the bottom, and two workmen in coveralls were on a bench facing the river, eating lunch.

"Never mind, that's how she'd do that," I said to Nas.

Rose approached the scaffolding like it was nothing more than the stairs leading up from the Métro. But a park security guard stepped between Rose and the scaffolding. "You can't go up there," he said.

Rose made an apologetic face and backed off. The guard walked away, toward some kids who were sitting in the middle of the bike path, blocking it.

I thought Rose would come back to brainstorm with me and Nas, but instead, she tilted her head, indicating Nas and I should come closer. When we got to her, she peered around, then handed one of the cleaning crew's buckets to me and one to Nas. She picked up a big brush and started to climb the scaffolding.

"Come on," she said. We couldn't wear our gala out-fits to go on the search for the next clue. That morning Nas had lent us some clothes so that we wouldn't need to slow down by stopping at our homes. Rose was wear-ing a pair of Nas's old basketball shorts and one of his sister's BTS T-shirts with the combat boots she always wore.

"I don't think we have a choice," I said to Nas. We heaved the buckets and followed her, trying not to slosh too much water out the tops.

My heart was racing, worried that we'd get caught. As he climbed behind me, Nas muttered, "I hate heights."

But Rose just charged forward and didn't seem at all worried about heights or the fact that we weren't even half-disguised as statue cleaners. She seemed to be oper-ating in "fake it till you make it" mode. We were doing really well at it because we managed to get all the way to the top of the scaffolding.

Once we got to the top, though, we had a problem.

"We can't reach the torch," Rose said. "See the little door? The clue must be inside there."

She was right. There was a tiny metal door on the torch, but it was about two feet higher than any of us could reach.

"I'm not touching that challenge," Nas said. He was clutching the metal railing and his voice was shaky.

"You're the tallest, Owen," Rose said. She'd noticed I was the tallest. That made me feel good.

I wanted to climb to the top of the copycat Statue of Liberty about as much as I wanted to go back to the Catacombs. But we'd made it this far, and I had this feeling I could do it. If Jules Verne had found a way to get up here to hide a clue inside the torch when he was an old man, couldn't I—a healthy thirteen-year-old who could do some really scary stuff on a skateboard—take whatever it was out?

"I'll get it," I said. I swung my leg over the statue's arm and climbed up, trying not to look down. The little door was kind of rusty—no wonder the statue needed cleaning—and I had to use my thumbnail to loosen it.

When it finally swung open, I could see a folded slip of paper nestled inside.

I reached to grab it and lost my grip on the statue's arm. I slid backward and yelled a swear in French (I was really good at remembering those).

"Regarde!" A little kid on the ground was pointing at me, but his mom was busy picking up after her small dog. I wished I had a water balloon to drop on him.

"I'll handle this, Owen," Rose said. She hissed something French to the kid in a sharp voice, and he said something that sounded like a taunt back. Meanwhile, just below me, Nas was clutching his stomach. "Can we hurry up?" he said to me.

I sucked in a breath and lunged forward to grab the paper. I yanked the folded square and toppled backward.

"Owen! No!" Nas said. I clutched the tiny slip of paper like it was going to be helpful to me as I fell seventy feet to the ground. Have I mentioned that I was also wearing a pair of Nas's old basketball shorts and one of his sister's BTS shirts? My death was going to be gruesome but also embarrassing.

I closed my eyes tight, waiting to hit the ground.

"Ooof." I landed hard, feeling a burst of air shoot from my lungs. Was I dead? I opened one eyelid. Rose and Nas were peering down at me. Nas was still gripping the railing with one hand and looked sicker than before.

By a miracle, I'd landed on the scaffolding and it broke my fall.

"Are you okay?" Rose said as she put her hand on my arm.

I tried to make words but the wind had been knocked out of me. I waved the small slip of paper weakly in front of my face.

"What are you doing?" Someone on the ground was yelling up at us. The security guy. He was running toward the statue, with the cleaning crew behind him.

"Let's go!" Rose said. She yanked my arm and pulled me to my feet. Wobbly, I started clattering down the scaffolding. Rose had to pry Nas's fingers from the rail to get him moving.

"It's worse going down than going up!" he said.

"We're almost there," I said. I was feeling steadier the closer I got to the ground, even though my shoulder hurt and my knee felt a bit banged up. We all jumped from the last level of the scaffolding onto the ground. A cluster of tourists startled and scattered as we landed.

"That way!" Rose said, pointing toward the bike path.

We sprinted toward it, dodging couples on tandem bikes and one guy in a whole Tour de France getup. My knee throbbed. We were putting space between us and the security guard, who looked ready to give up the chase.

We slowed down to catch our breath. "Let's get to the Métro," I said.

"Not so fast." The voice was familiar. Office Sad-face. He was jogging toward us from the opposite direction. Two other guys followed him.

"Run!" I said. We turned around and saw the park security guy pointing at us, as two more park security guards zoomed toward us on scooters.

We were surrounded.

CHAPTER THIRTY-ONE

On a Boat!

A SMALL ROWBOAT PASSED BY US IN THE RIVER JUST AHEAD of a bateau-mouche that was pulling away. Okay, we had one place to go.

"Follow me, guys," I said, running toward the Seine.

"To where? That's the river!" Nas yelped.

"We have to give ourselves up," Rose said.

"No, we don't! We need to get on a boat!" I raced toward the dock and jumped onto the bateau-mouche's deck.

A girl who was probably a year or two older than me screamed. Then she said, "Oh my god, do you like BTS, too?" in an American accent. I made a face like "of course" but then I circled around her toward the back of the boat.

"Come on," I yelled to Rose and Nas. "Make the jump!"

Rose must have known Nas would not be into this idea because she grabbed his arm and pulled him with her as she made a graceful, ballet-like leap onto the back of the boat. Nas was not so graceful, and hit the deck with his shoulder, rolling onto his side.

"You could have warned me!" he said to Rose.

"It's better you didn't think about it," she said.

"I would have done it," he said.

"You so would not have," Rose argued back.

A small crowd had gathered near us, and instead of freaking out, it sounded like they were taking sides in the Rose-Nas argument.

I was Team Rose, but before I could say this, I glanced up at the Grenelle bridge we were about to pass under. Officer Sadface was standing on top of it. I could tell he was looking for us on the boat, and then his eyes locked on mine.

"Where can we hide?"

"It's a boat with a giant open top deck," Nas said. "Nowhere!"

Now Sadface had his megaphone out and was telling people to move over on the deck of the boat. Two cops

in uniform behind him tossed rappels over the side of the bridge. They were going to lower themselves onto the deck! Tourists who'd been busy snapping photos of scenery started filming the cops.

"You're right," I said. I wove around a few tourists, cutting toward an open section of the boat. The cops were making their way down the rappels. We had maybe twenty seconds before their feet were on deck.

"Follow me," I said to Nas and Rose. My knee pulsed but I managed to sprint toward the railing and spotted a tugboat about ten feet down from where I stood. I climbed over the side of the railing and jumped, cradling my bag like a baby.

I tried to tuck and roll like I was bailing off my skateboard. I landed shoulder first, bending my arms and legs, so I side-somersaulted onto the deck, then skidded across it on my butt, and totally soaked my pants.

Rose and Nas followed my lead and slid toward me so we formed a heap. We scrambled to our feet as a man in galoshes came slip-sliding toward us, swatting us with the handle of his mop.

"Sorry, sir, sorry!" I yelled, getting to my feet and trying to dodge him as I ran along the slippery deck. The guy was still jabbing at us with the mop. I slid with both feet like I was snowboarding. My speed picked up as I coasted toward the side of the boat. I was not going to be able to stop. I half jumped, half fell over the railing and braced myself to hit water. But instead, I landed on a houseboat that was floating past.

"O! We're right behind you!" Nas said. He and Rose made intentional jumps onto the houseboat.

A woman who'd been sunbathing on top of the houseboat leaped up and screamed.

"Cassez-vous!" she yelled.

"Hey, that's 'get lost,' isn't it?" I asked my friends.

"We don't have time for language lessons, Owen," Rose said, running away from the lady, who tossed a magazine at us. I ducked to avoid it. She hurled a water bottle that missed Rose, and then her jar of suntan oil. It hit Nas on the elbow and exploded all over the three of us in a gooey coconut-scented blast.

As we dodged items, the cops were hurdling over the side of the tugboat, onto the houseboat.

Now the lady got really angry. "Sergio!" she screamed, and a huge man clambered up from a lower deck. When he saw the cops, his tan skin somehow turned an angry red and he pounded his fist into his palm. Then he growled at the cops, who started to back away. The woman picked up a beach umbrella and began swinging like bases were loaded. One of the cops staggered back and over the side of the boat, into the water. While the other two cops were helping him out and Sergio was lifting those guys off the ground by the collars of their shirts, Rose leaped off the deck and onto the banks of the Seine. Nas, who'd gotten suntan lotion in his eyes, somehow managed to slip away from the end of the umbrella that the lady was now swinging at us, and followed Rose.

"Nice meeting you," I said to the angry woman. Then I tossed the bag with the book and slip of paper inside to Rose and Nas and jumped just as the boat lurched under me. I braced myself to hit the ground, but instead, gravity kicked in early and I splashed into the water.

If it was actually water. The Seine water was gray and seemed dirty. As I surfaced, I spit a mouthful back into the river.

Rose was already reaching down. "Owen, here," she said. I spluttered toward her with a gross taste in my mouth. She and Nas helped yank me out of the river.

"Are you okay?" Nas said.

"I will be if we get out of here." We watched as Sergio hurled the other two cops off the boat into the water. They surfaced, spitting out mouthfuls of the Seine. They scowled at us and started to swim toward the banks of the river. "Right now," I said. "Let's go!"

CHAPTER THIRTY-TWO

Meet a Mime

Saturday, June 20, 12:30 p.m.

WE RUSHED TO THE NEAREST TINY ALLEY, WHERE I squeezed water out of my T-shirt and did my best to dump it from the Bête Noires. I was slightly less soaked as we turned down a busy street and ducked into a café. Not a nice café, but sort of an old, run-down one that wouldn't toss me outside for smelling like a dead sea creature from *Twenty Thousand Leagues Under the Sea*.

In a back booth of the diner, we ordered a plate of fries and Cokes for me and Nas, coffee for Rose. When

I felt a bit drier, I pulled the small piece of folded paper from inside the bag and opened it.

It was a ticket. From something called Deyrolle. "Wow! Deyrolle." Rose snatched the ticket from me.

"Deyrolle what?"

Rose seemed excited. "Finish the fries and let's go." She gave the ticket to Nas. "You're the driest. Put this in your pocket."

There were two mimes on our Métro ride to Deyrolle and when they saw me, dripping water onto the floor of the car, they seemed to agree on joining forces to make silent fun of me, which got a lot of not-silent laughs from the other passengers, and my friends.

The bigger mime pretended he wet his pants while the other one contorted his face to show what an embarrassing situation it was. Then they both waddled back and forth like they were the ones leaking water onto the floor.

I glared at the smaller mime as he joke-walked past me. "No one likes mimes anyway," I said.

The mime waddled up to me. He had a hand cupped to his ear like he hadn't heard what I said.

"I said, 'No one likes mimes anyway,'" I repeated.

The mime threw his head back silently and pretended to be bawling. A few people gave me dirty looks for hurting the mime's feelings and then handed the mime coins and bills. The mime took all their money and gave me a victorious smirk like he'd won a contest.

"Yeah, you're welcome," I said.

Now the mime was pretending to sing a serenade to me, which was somehow worse than when he'd been fake crying.

"Here's our stop," Rose said. "You're saved from more humiliation." Then she handed each mime a half-euro coin. "You did very well," she told them.

"At least in America, we make clowns join the circus," I said as we exited the car.

"Oh, so you know what you'll be doing for a living, then?" Rose joked.

Nas laughed. I rolled my eyes at Rose but I liked that she was teasing me playfully.

Up on the street, we made our way to the Deyrolle address. There were a lot of well-dressed people in this part of town and they gave the three of us odd looks. Rose and Nas had streaks of coconut suntan lotion on their oversized shirts and I was still smelly from the river.

When we finally arrived at Deyrolle, I was surprised. By the way Rose had said the name earlier, I'd been expecting a fancy department store. But from the outside, the Deyrolle building looked like an old piece of furniture, like Mrs. Fagerstadt's china cabinet, with dark brown wood framing its tall, gold-edged windows. A set of glass-and-wood double doors sat right in the center. It looked like a garden supply shop for people too rich to ever touch a garden tool. Brass and copper pots were stacked on top of each other, and I picked up one small garden spade and the price tag was as much as my uncle had sold his old convertible for. When I put it back with the others, all the spades began to fall to the floor.

"Acccck!" I yelled as I jumped back from the attacking garden implements. They landed with a crash.

From deep within the store, someone hissed, "Shhhhh!"

"Are you sure this is the right place?" I said. I tried to predict what the next thing I'd knock over would be. I was guessing the stacked pyramid of clay flowerpots.

But as I was predicting my future disasters, Rose and Nas had walked ahead to the back of the store. I saw their feet as they disappeared up a creaky spiral staircase to the second level.

"Hey, wait up!" I said, jogging up the steps as fast as I could. My knee didn't hurt as much now, but it was definitely going to bruise. I stumbled over one of the stairs near the top and crashed right into an angry boar with its teeth bared.

"Get away from me," I screamed, holding my arms up in front of my face like he was going to eat me. I lost my footing and tumbled slowly down the twisted staircase. My wet clothes sounded like a wet sponge being wrung out.

"Yep, it's really dead here today," Rose said. She and Nas were looking down at me from the top of the spiral. And that's when I realized the boar was taxidermied.

"Not funny," I said. I got to my feet and held on to the railing as I climbed up again. I made a point to stay as far from the boar as possible. It had an odd smell and was really creeping me out. But in trying to avoid the boar, I crashed into something furry and spun around. I was trapped in a bear hug, literally. The arms of a taxidermied black bear cub about my height had caught me. I hate to admit this, but I screamed again as I came face to furry face with its staring eyes, and I jumped backward.

"What is this place?" I said.

"Deyrolle," Rose said. "They sell items to a very specialized clientele."

"These are for sale?" I said.

Behind the bear were more taxidermied creatures, and none of them looked happy. A mean-faced hyena, prowling. A leopard, with an annoyed expression. A mama lion, glaring at me. An anteater whose long snout I tripped over as I backed away from the bear. I fell onto the floor, where I got a good view of its nostrils.

A whole wall was covered in frames containing dead bugs and butterflies pressed under glass. At least it was daylight outside. The idea of being in here at night made my stomach twist.

And the weirdest part was, there were people actually shopping. Some customers were using tiny magnifying glasses to inspect the wings of dead birds. A couple in matching jean jackets were comparing trays of beetles. A few of the shoppers shot me dirty looks as my wet shoes made squishing noises. I wondered if they wanted to add me to the collection of taxidermied animals.

"What is with this city and dead stuff?"

"You're not scared, are you, Owen?" Rose asked as she waggled a stuffed rat under my nose.

I stepped back, but only a little. "No. I'm just saying,

221

people might get the wrong idea about Paris."

Nas was looking at a drawer filled with colorful rocks and made a sarcastic noise. "O, if I can admit I'm afraid of heights, you can admit you're scared of dead stuff."

"Yeah, like you were cool with the BONE STAIRS," I shot back.

Rose laughed. "We don't have time for arguments. We should see if they still have whatever Jules left here for us."

"Oh, he's Jules now?" I said. "Shouldn't he at least be Uncle Jules or something?"

"Uncle Jules. Who maybe left us a bunch of treasure," Nas said.

He pulled the claim ticket from his pocket. "Who do you think we talk to about this? I don't see any salesclerks."

"May I help you?" a voice from behind Nas said. We spun around and could only see a massive polar bear with its teeth bared and a cold stare.

"Did that thing just talk to us?" Nas said, backing into me.

"Who's the baby now?" I asked.

"I don't know what there is to be afraid of," said a tiny old lady in a tweed jacket, stepping out from behind the bear. She had three mismatched silk scarves wrapped around her neck. "Now, can I help you?"

Rose plucked the ticket from Nas's hand and turned it over to the clerk. "We are hoping to pick up this item," she said.

The old lady squinted at the ticket but didn't say anything, just turned and started walking toward the back. She made a "Come on" gesture for us to follow her. Her fingers were covered in heavy rings with different colored gems. She disappeared around a corner and we hurried to keep up. She moved pretty fast for someone so weighed down by accessories. We passed more dead animals—naturally—and I tried to ignore the people who gave me angry looks for the trail of water I left on the wood floor. I was never going to dry off.

She led us to a big old wooden desk, half hidden by a gorilla that was beating its chest but had a semi-bored expression. Like it had been waiting at the desk for someone's help for way too long. The lady bypassed him and took a seat behind the desk, where she picked up a gold pen and flipped a page in a thick, handwritten ledger book.

Checking the number on our ticket, she flipped back even more pages, all the way to the front of the book. Then she scrunched her lips together and examined us. I got the feeling she would have been unimpressed with me even if I hadn't been sopping wet and smelly.

"Do you know if you still have it?" Rose asked,

nodding toward the ticket. Now the woman put on a pair of gold-rimmed glasses and held the ticket up to her face. She inspected the numbers again, like she was startled by how old the receipt was.

"It's a family heirloom," Rose said, lifting her arm to tuck a piece of hair behind her ear. Rose's watch, an antique silver chain-link bracelet with a small watch face at the center, slid down her arm. It stood out compared to the shorts and BTS shirt she had on. The clerk's gaze followed it, staring at the emeralds where the watch's 3, 6, 9, and 12 should have been. The clerk cleared her throat. "Well, you took your time picking this up," she said. "And as you may not know, we did suffer a fire some years ago. I can't guarantee the health of this item."

"Can it get much unhealthier than dead?" I joked. The lady didn't laugh.

Rose stepped in front of me and asked, "But surely it's worth checking?" She seemed way older than me and Nas at that moment, and almost like she was the boss of the lady behind the desk.

The lady nodded once. If she and Rose were in an ice-cold standoff, it would be hard to choose the winner. "We shall see." She stood up and disappeared through a small door behind the desk. We could hear her steps down a set of stairs.

A few minutes passed, and a puddle formed on the

floor under me. "Whatever she brings back, I have to go home and change before we try to figure it out," I said.

Nas nodded. "Yeah, me too."

Rose sighed. "Okay, fine," she said. "I guess it would be good to change clothes."

The clerk reappeared at the desk, wiping a cobweb from the shoulder of her jacket. She set a small packet onto the desk. I started to reach for it, but she held up a hand. "You owe"—she squinted at the receipt again—"one franc."

What was a franc? I reached into my pocket and pulled out a crumpled bill from the bottom. It was a five-euro note, wet and slimy. "Is this okay?"

The clerk turned away like she smelled something bad, which—to be realistic—she probably did. "Just sign here." She turned the massive ledger book toward me and flipped to a section in the back of lines of names.

I took the pen she handed me and paused. What if the cops came in here? At least right now, they didn't know my name. My mind was blank as I tried to come up with a good fake name.

But then one popped into my head.

In big, showy handwriting that looked nothing like my usual signature, I wrote *C. Nemo*.

CHAPTER THIRTY-THREE

Not Just Any Saturday Afternoon

Saturday, June 20, 2:15 p.m.

WE LEFT DEYROLLE AND WALKED INTO A DIFFERENT DAY than the one it had been when we entered the store. It had been sunny and warm just twenty minutes ago, but now a cool wind was blowing and the blue sky had been replaced with clumps of gray clouds. My damp clothes stuck to my body and made me feel clammy. I really needed a shower. It wasn't that late, but we'd already done a lot for the day and I wanted to check in with my mom.

But I still wanted to see what was in the package. We all did.

When we were a block away, the three of us huddled together around the corner from Deyrolle to open the package. The paper-wrapped parcel was tied with twine that was fraying and rough. I used the edge of my thumb to tease out the knot and worked the rest of the twine loose until I could separate it from the paper. Rose lifted the corner of the brown paper and pulled it to reveal a velvet pouch about the size of a large marble. Nas carefully picked up the pouch and held it in his palm.

"O, you open it," he said. "You got it." I held the bottom of the pouch with one hand and tugged loose the drawstring holding it closed. I could tell from feeling the bag that whatever was inside was hard and cylindric, and pointed at the ends. Maybe a diamond, I thought.

I shook the object out of the bag and looked at what was in my palm.

"A rock? What are we going to do with a rock?" I blurted through chattering teeth. Because that's what it was. Not a diamond but a transparent, green-tinged rock. Like something you'd buy at a museum gift shop. And not for much money.

Rose pinched it with two fingers. "It's not a rock. It's a crystal." The sun was mostly blocked by a cloud, but Rose stepped into a small patch of sunlight on the

227

sidewalk and held the crystal up to the weak ray. The sun filtered through the crystal and made droplets of light dance on the gray sidewalk. But that was it. No Jules Verne hologram projected itself onto the street and said, "Yo, the real treasure is at the Bank of France and here's an account number." Which, maybe I'd kind of been hoping for.

All at once, I felt tired. I had no idea what to do with a rock. Or a crystal. I'd survived the Catacombs, climbed a statue, been chased down the river, and been to a weird store filled with dead animals. I'd thought we'd fulfilled our quests.

Plus, the longer this took, the more time it gave whoever had foul-played Professor Bessier to find us. The cops were already after us. How much time did we have before the bad guys were, too?

I shivered a little, partly from being wet and in the shade, and partly because I had that feeling again of being watched.

"I really should go home for a while," I said. "My mom's probably waiting for me." Who knew if that was true, but it was strange that she hadn't even texted me yet today. Rose and Nas were complaining about having to deal with their pushy parents, and that only made my mom forgetting me feel even worse.

"Should we check in later?" Nas said.

Rose nodded and handed me the crystal. "Can you hold on to this? Keep it with the medallion and the book."

"Sure," I said. Nas lightly tossed me the bag and I caught it and slung the strap over my shoulder.

"I'd better go," he said. "I'm already late."

Rose's phone pinged. She glanced at the message. "My dad is wondering where I am. I better go, too."

We said goodbye and they both walked off in the opposite direction from me. I hoped my mom would be waiting when I got home. Maybe she'd tried to text and hadn't been able to get a signal. She might even be worried. Then I could tell her about the medallion, the book, and the crystal while she made us pasta.

I walked quickly the whole way back. I raced up the stairs to our walk-up and got excited when I saw the door partway open. Mom was always forgetting to close the door all the way. She was kind of the definition of an absent-minded professor.

But when I slipped inside, a terrible smell hit my nose. It smelled like the time Hudson Travers threw a plastic squirt gun into a bonfire at Darren Leach's house. "Mom?" I said, the cold inside my stomach turning to a hot, nervous lava. "Mom?" I said it a little louder and stepped carefully into the apartment, checking every corner of the small room as I entered. I knew something was wrong. My legs wobbled beneath me.

The smell was coming from the kitchen. Right away I saw the ingredients for my mom's pepper-and-oil baked chicken—my favorite—on the counter, and when I opened the oven, I saw the chicken, or what was left of it. The baking pan was filled with chicken bones and black ash that had once been the meat. I didn't know how no one had smelled it. My mom's phone was on the counter, and I reached out to tap it awake. No new messages. I looked at the voice mail. She'd listened to my message from the night before.

She must have started cooking for me and Rose and Nas when something—or someone—interrupted her. Maybe it was an emergency at the lab, I told myself. Maybe she'd just run out to handle an emergency and forgotten to shut things off. There was a bowl of cacio e pepe on the table where the escargot pizza had been, the cheesy sauce all congealed and the noodles clumped together. It was my other favorite, but you had to eat it pretty soon after it was prepared. On the old tile floor was spilled grated cheese, like a dusting of snow. There were treads in the cheese—a sneaker, like my mom's. *Lab emergency lab emergency lab emergency*, I repeated to myself, thinking if I said it enough, it would be true. But then, closer to the door was another dusting of cheese, and in that one was half a print from a large boot. Not my mom's boot. Maybe the kind of boot someone who

230

wore a trench coat and stalked kids looking for Jules Verne's treasure would wear. A foul-play boot.

A piece of paper stuck out from under the pasta bowl. With my teeth gritted, I pulled it along the table closer to me and flipped it over. My arms felt as stringy as the noodles as I lifted it up to read the writing. There was an address and a time, 9:30 p.m., and today's date. And then the message.

We have your mom. Bring the book.

CHAPTER THIRTY-FOUR

It Gets Worse

I DROPPED THE NOTE BACK ONTO THE TABLE AS A CLUMPY ache hit my lungs. I clawed my inhaler out of my pocket and pumped it into my mouth, hoping that when I could breathe again, my mom would be there and I'd figure out this was all a bad dream. She'd just be finishing making chicken and pasta and we'd eat together and talk about how crazy the last few days have been.

I sucked in air, untangling the thick noodle knot in my chest. I breathed oxygen, but the air tasted ashy and dry from the charred chicken.

And my mom was still gone. The scary footprint was still there.

This was all my fault.

I grabbed the edge of the table, taking deep breaths. Then I was back in Connecticut.

"Owen, can you come in here and grind some pepper?"

A Frank Sinatra song spilled out over our kitchen. Mom's favorite Italian Cooking Music playlist.

Mom was at the stove wearing her favorite, Kiss the Scientist; Our Cooking Gets Reactions *apron and stirring some pasta water into a pot of bucatini. She handed me the pepper mill as she dumped in a bowl of grated cheese. "Lots of pepper, or it's not cacio e pepe."*

My mouth started to water when I saw the pasta and smelled the pan of juicy chicken that was resting on the table. I cranked the grinder, watching slivers of pepper rain down onto the pasta. Mom lifted and stirred the noodles so each strand was properly coated with the cheesy-peppery mixture.

"What movie are we watching again?" I asked.

"Back to the Future," Mom said. "My favorite."

"Isn't that from the nineties?"

"It's from 1985, thank you very much. It's a classic."

"You know, there are perfectly good movies made in just the last year. There's been a lot of progress in special effects. Don't you think a scientist should want to see realistic visuals?"

Mom bumped me with her hip and turned the pot of

cacio e pepe into her favorite red bowl with the image of a rooster on it—a yard sale find from last summer. "Nice try," she said. "How about this? If you don't like the movie, you can pick the next one. If you do, I get to pick everything we watch this weekend."

I grinned. "I guess, since it was your idea to hold Mom and Owen's Super-Jammed, Super-Awesome, All-You-Can-Eat Weekend Movie Marathon, that's fair."

Mom set out plates and I grabbed napkins. "That's the correct answer. I always knew you were a genius."

"Takes one to raise one."

"Let's eat."

CHAPTER THIRTY-FIVE

I Have to Fix This

Saturday, June 20, 4:50 p.m.

I OPENED MY EYES. MY BODY WAS BENT OVER AND MY forehead was against the table edge, like I'd fallen asleep standing up. But if I'd been asleep, I wasn't rested. I must have fainted.

I knelt to the floor and felt tears start flowing from my eyes, until my whole body was shaking and I couldn't stop crying. Across the room, I saw the shape of the book inside the messenger bag. None of this would have happened if it weren't for that stupid book.

Nope, it wasn't the book's fault. It was mine.

One of the things my mom studied in her lab was chaos theory. The simplest way to explain it is that every little thing that happens is linked to everything else, and one tiny random thing can throw off or kickstart some other major event. It's also called the butterfly effect, because of a Chinese proverb: "The slight flutter of the wings of a butterfly can be felt on the other side of the world." It's supposed to be a reminder that nothing is predictable, and one small thing someplace can change a big event someplace else. But in my case, I could see the chain clearly.

I had been upset that my mom didn't read my *Great Expectations* paper, so I'd ripped it up and gotten the lousy grade that got me put in this seminar. And because of the seminar, I had embarrassed myself in front of Rose, then tried to make up for that by talking to her at Le Dôme, leaving my backpack to be stolen by that twerp, and losing the book. The book I replaced with the idiotic prophecy book that someone thought was so valuable it was worth kidnapping my mom.

I pushed away from the table and stomped toward the bag. I shook the book out onto the floor and kicked it across the room. It flopped open to another page full of nonsense. Why hadn't I left it alone?

"The only prophecy in here is that you ruined my life." I tore the page out and shredded it into smaller pieces. This book was bad news and needed to be destroyed.

I tore a second page out and ripped that one up, too.

I grabbed the corner of a third page and paused to wipe my wet face with my hand. This wasn't going to do any good. I couldn't hurt a stupid book the way I thought it had hurt me.

Plus…the book was the only way I'd get my mom back.

I stopped tearing and folded up the torn pages. I shoved them into my pocket.

Whoever wanted this book could have it. I didn't care if it led to some amazing treasure that Jules Verne had hidden. Nothing was worth losing my mom.

I imagined handing the book over to someone in all black—the person or people who'd been following us. I imagined my mom, relieved and proud that I'd saved her. I imagined everything getting better after that. I'd be happy to have a completely boring summer full of seminars and even sitting in a library while my mom lectured if it meant she was safe, and I still had a mom.

But if the kidnappers had the book, what happened next? If they were evil enough to drag my mom from the apartment, maybe they wanted whatever was in the prophecy for an equally bad reason. Or, maybe a worse than equally bad reason. What if they wanted to use the treasure to hurt more people, or start the apocalypse? Maybe that's why Bessier had gone missing. Someone thought he had the book and had kidnapped him, too. Or maybe it was Bessier who'd taken my mom, and he was trying to get it back.

He'd been awfully careful with the book that night. He'd locked it in his secret cabinet and taken another book to meet with those people in the car. A decoy book.

I didn't know if Bessier was a good guy or a bad guy in this situation, but I knew he wasn't stupid.

I'd get a decoy book, too. I'd trade it for my mom, and then hide the real book. Or destroy it.

Unless the bad guy was Bessier, who'd seen the real book. He'd know if I handed him a decoy. Something told me, though, that he wasn't the one who'd left the note and taken my mom.

My eyes fell on the giant boot print on the floor. I thought maybe I should call the police. But, for all I knew, the police were in on it. Treasure was treasure, and just because you were supposed to be a good guy didn't mean you were always good. I'd seen enough movies to know that.

I had to handle this myself.

And to do that, I had to move to the next link of the chain of events I'd started. I had to get my mom back.

CHAPTER THIRTY-SIX

We Hit the Books

WITH A PLAN IN MIND, I WAS ABLE TO CALM DOWN AND get dressed. It was early Saturday evening and the time on the note said to meet at the address at 9:30 p.m. Even though I worried a little that the kidnapper could see my messages, I had to tell someone what was going on. I texted Rose and Nas.

Someone took my mom. They want the book. But I don't think we should give it to them. Where can I get an old book that no one will notice? (Not from Rose's dad or a bookstore...somewhere low-key.)

I sounded sure of myself in the text, which was good, because I didn't feel that way one bit.

Nas and Rose replied quickly.

Nas: Your mom is missing? Are you okay? Should we call the police?

Rose: OMG, Owen. It's going to be okay. Maybe Nas is right. We can let the police handle this.

I wrote back: We don't know if the police are on our side. We just need a book.

There was a long pause and the three dots. I held my breath.

Rose: You're right. Okay, a book. Meet at the Bibliothèque Nationale de France. (Not the new one; the reading room on Rue de Richelieu.)

Nas: My parents just got home and I'm off sibling watch. I'll say we're sleeping over at your place. I'm so sorry this happened. I should have been watching your backpack better that day.

Poor Nas. I hadn't even thought he might feel as bad as I did. So I wrote, Not your fault. Thanks for coming to help me.

💀 💀 💀

The cold wind from earlier was gone now, and the day was sunny and warm again. I wore my darkest jeans and T-shirt and a hat pulled low over my face. From under the brim, I watched everyone I passed on my way to the Bibliothèque Nationale. My heart jumped up every time I saw a woman with dark hair, or a gray jacket like my mom's favorite one. But none of the people were her. She was really missing, and if I wanted to find her, I had to keep my focus. I'd learned that from watching movies, too.

Rose and Nas were already waiting for me under a peaked doorway with a large clock set into the stone. It reminded me a bit of the clock tower in *Back to the Future*, which reminded me of Mom, and I had to gulp to stop from crying again. When my friends saw me, they raced down the steps and tackled me on either side in a huge hug.

"I wanted to bring you a good luck charm," Rose said. She pressed a tiny golden heart into my hand. "It's from one of my mother's necklaces. I used to sleep with it under my pillow when I had bad dreams. I know, it's stupid."

"No, it's not," I said. "But I can't take one of your mom's things."

"I want you to have it," Rose said.

"Thank you," I said. I put it deep into my pocket. Rose leaned toward me and hugged me. When we pulled apart, I saw her eyes were a little wet, like she'd been crying, too, and it felt nice to think that someone cared about me. Without Nas and Rose, there was no way I'd be able to get through this.

"You sure you don't want to call the police? Or a detective or something?" Nas said. "This is kind of serious, isn't it?"

I already had an answer ready. "My mom hasn't even been missing for a whole day. If we have to wait around for cops, it could take forever, and who knows what will happen?"

Now I turned to Rose. "You think they'll have a book here?"

Rose grinned. "This place is filled with strange old books, and they're easier to get to than the old books at the new national library. I think they'll have a lot of decoy books. And it's a library, so no one will notice if one's missing. We just need to choose the one that will fool the person who wants our book."

We walked inside, and the smell of old books—paper and dust—hung in the air. A chandelier made from hundreds of droplet-shaped pieces of glass dangled above us and caught the sun coming through the windows, spilling fragments of light over the white walls and floor. Rose led us down a hallway and into the main reading room.

"Whoa," I said. The buildings in Paris kept one-upping each other for most impressive insides. The reading room was a large open space beneath a ceiling composed of dozens of domes, each with a circular skylight at its center. In every spot where four domes met, a giant white column ran from the floor to ceiling. The pillars looked like the huge bones of a prehistoric animal, but the room itself felt more like being inside a hollowed-out wedding cake. Books lined the walls, but most of the room was filled with rows of desks, many of them filled with people at work. I counted at least twenty signs that said SILENCE, S'IL VOUS PLAÎT! Meaning they really wanted you to be quiet in French libraries.

"I didn't tell you earlier, but this is the library where Jules Verne used to work," Rose said. "I know you might not want to hear that name right now, but technically, he didn't kidnap your mom."

"Well, have we ruled out time travel?" I said. It was a joke my mom would have liked.

"If he time-traveled, it was only to get ideas for all the crazy stuff in his books," Nas said.

"You've got a point," I said. "Though you'd think he'd erase the stuff about fax machines." I was glad to be joking around. It made things feel almost normal, and normal was what I wanted right now.

Rose walked ahead of us, very aware of where she was going. "There's a section of reference books from the turn of the century that will be good for a decoy,"

243

she said. "We should find something as close in size and color to our prophecy book as we can. The kidnappers may have an idea of what it looks like."

"Especially if they've been trailing us," I said. "Like whoever was chasing me at the Catacombs."

"Yeah, ever since you texted, I've been extra creeped out," Nas said. "Like, what if they don't stop with your mom?"

He glanced from me to Rose, and I could tell he was worried about his parents and the rest of his family.

"I know my dad gets on my nerves, but I wouldn't be able to think straight if he were missing," Rose said. She patted my arm. "I admire you, Owen."

While I liked when Rose teased me for being an American, it was nice to hear her say that. I didn't think I deserved to be admired at all—it was my fault my mom was missing—but that wasn't Rose's fault.

Nas was bobbing his head up and down like he was listening to music on his headphones, but they were around his neck. I realized he was doing a count of how many people were in the library. The main room was crowded with people working at desks and walking up and down the aisles.

"It's kind of busy here, at least a hundred fifty peo-ple," he said, smiling politely at a library page pushing a cart of books past us. "Maybe I should keep watch while you guys look for the book."

I nodded, trying not to get openly sad again as I thought about how much my mom would have loved this place.

"Yes, that's a good plan," Rose answered Nas. "The library will be closing soon. We should work fast," she added.

"Don't get in trouble," Nas said.

I tried to keep my voice upbeat as I replied, "Too late for that."

Not Quiet in the Library

NAS WANDERED OVER TO THE STUDY CARRELS AND DESKS, leaning against empty ones every so often as he scanned the library. He was trying so hard to be low-key that he was being a little high-key instead, but at least most of the library patrons were engaged in their work and didn't pay him much attention.

I was crouched near the floor, reading the bindings of books on a low shelf. Rose was a few feet away on a stool, tipping books back from the shelves and sliding them back into place when they didn't meet her standards.

"What about this one?" I said, showing Rose a greenish book that was about the right width.

She shook her head. "That's too new."

"Oh," I said. I put the book back. Rose seemed way more sure of what we needed to find than I was, so I stepped away from the shelves to see how Nas was doing.

Nas was the only person in the library wearing an oversized hoodie and giant headphones. He looked like he'd walked in from DJing a party and gotten lost on the way to the bathroom. His head twisted left and right like he was watching a Ping-Pong match as he made sure no one came to bother me and Rose. Nas spotted me and waved across the library as he walked behind some people working at two desks next to each other. Then he stopped at a desk that was slightly different from the rest and roped off from the others. Nas leaned over the velvet rope to read something on a triangular sign. He pointed at the desk and mouthed something.

"What?" I mouthed back.

Nas whispered something but I couldn't make it out. I shook my head, to let him know he could tell me later.

But then he said, loud enough for me and the people around him to hear, "It's Jules Verne's desk. He worked here!" Half the room glanced up from their work to shoot him dirty looks.

"Tell him to be quiet!" Rose mouthed dramatically as she held a book in each palm, like she was literally weighing her options.

"Shhh!" I hissed back at Nas, annoyed. We had more important things to do than turn this into some kind of Jules Verne field trip. And I didn't want to get kicked out of the library before we got what we needed.

But instead of taking the hint to leave the desk alone, Nas sat down at it. Jules Verne's desk! Then, as if that wasn't bad enough, he pulled on his headphones and ran his hands over the top of the desk, then with two fingers, started to scratch an imaginary record on it, like the desk was a DJ table. His head was bobbing to his music and then he added his own bassline to his fake scratches, making a loud "OUUNSA-OUUNSA-OUUNSA" noise with his mouth.

Everyone in a twenty-foot radius stopped to watch as Nas did a whole set, pretending to flip records off and on the turntables, all while layering in more of his own sounds. Most of the people looked pretty annoyed, but a few who'd turned to stare were smirking and enjoying the show. A couple of people started filming on their phones. I got nervous. If the video went viral and the people who had my mom saw it, they'd figure out what we were doing.

I was about to run over and tell him to cut it out before he got us kicked out or worse, but then his set must have ended and Nas looked up, like he'd had no idea what he'd been doing or even that he was in a library.

I breathed a sigh of relief, peeking to see if Rose had made any progress, but when I made a "What's up?" gesture to her, she shook her head at the book she was holding and shoved it back on the shelf.

I turned back to Nas, to make sure he hadn't started a new set. And, as I was watching, he started to tug at the handle of the desk's small drawer! Now the people next to him who'd been patient with his record spinning glared with expressions that seemed to say, "You should not mess around with Jules Verne's desk." Really, it's an unspoken rule that anything old and behind velvet ropes with a special sign on it is kind of in the "Don't mess with this!" category.

I thought about throwing something at him, but I didn't want to cause any more commotion than Nas already was. I'd help Rose instead, so we could get out of here faster. I grimaced at the shelves of books, pulling out a greenish one that might work only to see it was the same book I'd shown to Rose before.

Back by the desks, Nas was still trying to open the drawer and I didn't understand why. He rattled it loud enough that I could hear it across the library. He must have been listening to music through his headphones, because he didn't seem to notice that people were getting angry. They were shushing him and muttering French curse words in his direction. The irritation rippled out from Nas's position across the library floor.

I started to head for him, hissing "Nas!" but he was so obsessed with the drawer he didn't hear me. He took our prophecy book out of his lap and set it on the desk, so he could try the drawer again with both hands.

My heart was pounding and my stomach felt like it was on fire from the inside. He was stressing me out.

The book started to slide down the desk's slanted top, and if it hit the floor, it would definitely make a distracting noise. Nas didn't even notice it as he bent forward in the chair, still rattling the drawer. I stood motionless as the book inched down the desktop, bracing myself

for the noise of it falling. But then it stopped its journey and clicked into a groove on the desk's surface, sort
of how Bessier's slippers had clicked into the notches in
his floor.

Out of nowhere, a metal piece on the back of the desk
began to lift up, as if a crank was being turned under the
desk. Nas reeled back away from the drawer, pushing
his chair out from under the desk and popping to his
feet. The studiers next to him lurched away, staring at
the desk as the metal plate unfolded itself and covered
the book. Nas scrambled toward the book and began
to push at the edge of the metal plate. I felt paralyzed,
watching the whole mess. Nas tried to claw underneath
the metal plate, which had enveloped the book like
wrapping paper.

"We should get out of here," the studiers said, as
two other people who'd been waiting for a seat pointed
at Nas and whispered to each other. They started to
speed-walk toward the information desk at the front of
the room.

Nas was grunting as he kept wrestling with the desk,
and the mechanical sounds of the gears mixed with his
frustrated noises.

"What are you doing?" a man with a thick beard
said. He slammed his book shut and started to stand up.

Nas shook his head, huffing and puffing as he tried prying the metal piece away from our book, and looked over to me. "Owen, help! The desk is taking our book!"

I came unfrozen. The book. We needed the book if I was going to get Mom back.

And Jules Verne's desk was about to steal it from us.

CHAPTER THIRTY-EIGHT

The Prophecy Didn't See This Coming

A LIBRARIAN HAD STOOD UP FROM THE LARGE ROUND counter at the far end of the room. The two patrons who'd tattled were watching as the librarian charged toward Nas and me. We locked eyes and I smiled sheepishly but instead of smiling back, she set her face in an even angrier expression.

I ignored her and tried to help Nas. I grabbed at the metal plate he was fighting with. I gritted my teeth and worked to slide my hand underneath it to pull the book out, but the plate folded itself again, encasing the book on all sides. Nas and I both tried to push or pull against the strange device, but some gear beneath the desk kept turning with a rusty cranking noise. Finally, I jumped on top of the desk, fighting against it, but battling the desk was like playing tug-of-war against a pro wrestler. The machinery yanked the book backward, away from me. I gritted my teeth and pulled as the library patrons started to come toward us with angry expressions, but the machine worked with so much force, it sent me flying backward off the desk. I landed against the velvet rope, and the two brass stands holding it toppled and clanged loudly against one another.

Then the book, inside the metal wrapping paper, disappeared somewhere inside the desk. "Oh no!" I yelled. If the book was gone, how would I help my mom? I felt tears come into my eyes again and bent my head so no one would see.

"What on earth are you doing, standing on Mr. Verne's desk?" the librarian said.

"Nothing, ma'am," Nas said. "We're sorry about the noise."

I was trying to avoid making eye contact with anyone when the desk made a ding behind Nas's back and a drawer slid out. I sprang to my feet, blocking the inside of the drawer from the librarian's view. "I'm so sorry, it was stupid of me. It won't ever happen again," I said. I glanced down at the drawer. Inside was a pair of bronze eyeglasses.

It had to be a clue. It wasn't about the treasure any-more, but if there were clues to get, I thought it was bet-ter if we had them than if the kidnappers did.

"We won't bother anyone else," I added. I used the polite voice I did when Mom took me with her to fancy work events. The librarian must have been convinced because she left in a huff.

When she'd made it back to her desk, I tapped Nas's shoulder. I pointed at the glasses. He picked them up and immediately tried them on.

He turned his head from side to side, then he held his hand in front of his face, squinting through the lenses. "Whatever these things are, they're not going to do us any good," he said. "Our man Jules Verne had messed-up eyesight. Everything's blurry."

I pulled them off his nose and put them in a side pocket of the bag. "Doesn't matter, I'm keeping them," I said. "Let's try to get the book. Quietly."

I sat at the desk and Nas walked over to the other side of it. I got up and got another book off the shelf, laying it in the groove where our book had been, to see if the desk would try to eat any book. But nothing happened.

"This isn't working," I said, trying not to let myself worry too much. The whole point of being here was to get a decoy book to give the kidnappers, so maybe it was okay if we didn't have the original.

"I'm sorry, O," Nas said. "I thought maybe I'd find something helpful, not screw everything up."

I shrugged. "Maybe it's better this way," I said. "I think *La Prophétie* is gone."

"Nope, it's right here," came Rose's voice behind me. I spun around and she was holding a green-covered book that I knew wasn't *La Prophétie* but that definitely convinced me it was, as long as I didn't look too closely. I had a good feeling that the kidnappers would believe it was the real thing, too.

Or at least I hoped they would. Because even though we'd come here for a decoy, in the back of my head, I had felt like as long as I had the real book, I'd have something to trade to get my mom back.

I checked the big clock ticking over the library, which was quiet again. I gave the desk one long last look, too, hoping maybe it would eject the prophecy book. But the book wasn't coming out.

"We have to be at the rendezvous soon," I said. "Let's go."

CHAPTER THIRTY-NINE

Time for Fireworks

Saturday, June 20, 9:28 p.m.

THE MEETING SPOT WASN'T FAR, BUT IT FELT A MILLION years away from the fancy library. It was the first building I'd seen in Paris that was a boring brick box, with small windows high up on its outer walls, and no decoration on the outside except for the numbers in its address, which were painted above a metal garage door that seemed to be the only entrance. The sun was starting to go down, and a light breeze was blowing, casting wavy shadows on the building that kept making me think someone was walking toward us.

"Are you sure this is it?" Nas said.

"The address is right. We must have to go inside."
I put my sneaker under the bottom of the garage door
and raised my foot. The door rolled up partway. "And I
guess this is the way to get in."

We ducked under the opening, and I pulled the door
down behind us. We were in a loading area of some sort.
On every side, tall stacks of wooden crates formed a
maze. A little light came in from another open roll-up
door on the opposite side of the cavernous space. I shivered, wondering if the kidnappers were already here.
But it was silent.

"It looks like it's a fireworks factory," Rose said,
studying a far wall. Unlike the drab gray walls outside,
this wall was painted with a huge mural of fireworks
exploding over Paris. The scene was weirdly familiar,
and then I remembered the fireworks the night at the
Musée des Arts et Métiers. The party felt like it had
happened years ago, not the night before.

"So all these boxes are filled with fireworks?" Nas
said, reading the side of one crate that said RED ROCKETS
and another that said BLUE DEMONS. He shook his head.
"Seems like someone should tell them this is a major fire
hazard."

I checked my phone. No service, but the clock
worked. "They're late," I said. My stomach twisted as I

259

wondered if I had the wrong place. Or, worse, if something had changed and the kidnappers didn't have my mom to trade.

"Do you think they're hiding somewhere?" Rose said. "There's that other door. What if they're inside?" She crept quietly between two tall stacks of crates, toward the open door at the other side. Nas and I followed on tiptoe.

We went deeper into the maze of crates and stepped out into an empty bit of floor, with long, low-slung tables covered with firework insides—casings and wrappers and wicks. I was looking around for signs that someone had been here when a gray sedan turned into the open garage door.

I jumped back, knocking into Rose and Nas.

Then Rose's dad got out of the driver's seat.

"Dad? What are you doing here?" Rose's voice was shakier than I'd ever heard it. I understood. My head went light for a second as the knowledge flashed in my mind.

"Where's my mom? Tell me now!" I balled up my fists and charged at him. But Rose's dad was stronger than he looked, and he simply grabbed me by the shoulders, stopping me before I could look in the car. Over my head, as I fought against his grip, he asked Rose, "What is he talking about?" Now he stared into my face.

I glared right back at him. "Your friend Owen is a thief! He has stolen something very valuable. We are trying to help solve this without involving the authorities."

"I'm not a thief!" Unless he meant the glasses we'd just taken? But how would he know that? "You're trying to trick Rose. You took my mom! Where is she?" I said, out of breath. I wasn't sure if it was another asthma attack coming on or just my anger.

"Owen didn't steal anything," Nas said.

"He has an extremely valuable book that he took from the Musée des Arts et Métiers last night," Rose's dad said. "I have the information from a trusted source."

He must have meant the prophecy book. But who was the trusted source? The cop? One of those Jules Verne Society people? Who would say I stole anything?

Rose put a hand on her dad's hand, and his fingers loosened enough that I was able to wrench one arm out of his grasp. "Dad, Owen didn't steal that book. We bought it. I was there."

Now the passenger door of the car opened, and LaForge stepped out. She looked like she was dressed for a nice dinner at a hip café, in a blouse and jeans with cowboy boots. Over it, she had on a purple coat. "Owen," she said in a soft voice, smiling kindly at me. "The book you stole, it's very valuable. You must take responsibility."

She took a soft step toward me and reached out a hand. "Is the book in that bag? Why don't you hand it to me?"

There was something about her that was different. Her eyes were gleaming as she looked past me at the messenger bag.

And that's when it hit me: I'd seen that coat before.

In the Catacombs!

The person who'd tried to steal the medallion from me was wearing a purple coat.

But LaForge had helped me that day. My mind was racing as I tried to sort everything out.

"The book is valuable and you shouldn't have taken it. And the medallion you stole," she said. "They are property of the Musée des Arts et Métiers. And you know Rose's father is a benefactor to the museum, and he wouldn't want one of his daughter's friends to do something damaging."

Monsieur Bordage smiled, almost sympathetically. "Chantal had mentioned that you're left alone a lot, but that is no reason to do something so delinquent. Please return the artifacts."

Rose motioned with her arms. "Dad, Owen took nothing. You have to believe me. We *bought* the book." She pointed at LaForge. "You can't trust her."

Nas nodded vigorously.

LaForge knew about the medallion. It *had* been her that day at the Catacombs. She smiled at me like she knew a secret I didn't.

I remembered how interested in the book she'd seemed earlier. And she was a Jules Verne scholar, too. Of course she'd want the book. But still, why hadn't she just asked? Why would she do all this to get a book? And was she behind Bessier's disappearance?

Rose had been right to treat LaForge like she had. All at once, I knew I shouldn't have trusted LaForge.

I held the bag in front of me but clutched it with both hands, like I was protecting it. "First, tell me where my mom is. I know you know."

LaForge laughed lightly. "I'm sure your mother is just working." Then, more sharply, she said to me, "Let's not make your problems worse. You have two things that belong to me...the medallion. And the book."

Nas put his hand on my shoulder, as if he could tell I was close to shaking with anger. "Where's his mom?"

Rose squeezed her dad's hand. "Dad, she's lying. Owen didn't steal anything."

Then, more quietly, Rose said, "We don't have the book. Not right now, anyway." Rose gave LaForge a longer look that was almost nice. "We can tell you where the book is, but only if you can bring us Owen's mother."

LaForge seemed to be listening, but her face gave

away nothing. "For years, I've worked to be known as the foremost Jules Verne scholar. And for even longer than that, I've heard whispers of a lost book of his that might tell of something extraordinary that Jules Verne hid, right here in Paris. I took those whispers seriously," she said. Moonlight was falling through the open garage door that made it look like LaForge was in a spotlight for all of this. "So seriously, in fact, that many of my colleagues made me a laughingstock. Even Professor Bessier. He never believed me. And then I learned that he got his hands on the book I've believed in all these years. The book that might lead to unpublished works, or hidden artifacts, or perhaps even clues to how Verne wrote what he did. To see this book in the hands of some kids is infuriating. So I did what I had to do." She looked at me.

"Your mother is safe. For now," she said. "But I will need the book." She reached out and cupped my chin in her hand. Her fingers were ice cold. She squeezed a little. "Owen, I think you'd like to help me."

I gulped. "I would…," I said, even though the idea that someone would hurt my mom, and maybe Bessier, too, for a book was terrifying. She might have started out wanting to be a Jules Verne scholar but she'd turned into something else along the way. "We lost the book. We can try to help you find it, but I'm going to need my mom first."

Hearing that, LaForge's smile fell away. She clenched her jaw and squeezed my face so that her nails dug into my skin painfully. I winced.

"Oh, you think it's that simple?"

She pushed me backward.

"I tried to make this pleasant for you."

CHAPTER FORTY

It Gets Real

I was stumbling backward and off balance when LaForge lunged at me. She grabbed the strap of the bag and tore it from my arm. I flew away from her and landed sprawled on the ground. I winced as pain reappeared in the shoulder I'd fallen on earlier.

She spun away from us, protecting the bag like a wounded animal. Rose got a grip of LaForge's upper arm and yanked on it but LaForge shoved her backward, knocking Rose into Nas and sending them both to the ground.

Rose's dad had been watching LaForge toss us all aside with a more and more horrified expression. Now he took steps toward her, saying, "Chantal, I don't know what's going on but I think there must be some mistake." As he got closer, he extended his hand as if he wanted to comfort her, but LaForge shoved his arm away with her side. He lost his balance and fell to the floor face-first.

With all of us at different stages of trying to get up, LaForge reached inside the bag and pulled out the decoy book. She had a cruel grin on her face as she shook the empty messenger bag.

"Where is the medallion?" she asked, not even trying to hide that she'd been the one trying to steal it from me at the Catacombs.

Lying as if my life depended on it, because maybe it did, I said, "Lost in the Seine." In truth, Nas, Rose, and I had each hidden the medallion, the crystal, and the glasses from the library within our clothing. I had the medallion inside my shoe. Rose had stowed the crystal inside a small pocket of her skirt, and Nas had the glasses in an inner pouch of his hoodie. I was relieved we'd taken the time to protect those things.

"Figures you'd lose it," LaForge said. "But no matter." Clutching the book greedily, she tossed the empty messenger bag to me.

I caught it, holding my breath while she flipped through the decoy book's pages.

She hadn't really seen the real book we'd had at Rose's house. Maybe it would actually fool her and this could all be over.

"Do you think it's so easy to fool me?" She slammed the book shut and hurled it deep into the warehouse. Her face contorted with anger as she spun on us. "Where is the real book? The book you had before? *La Prophétie de Jules Verne!*"

I made her wait for me as I got to my feet and brushed the dust from my clothes. I wasn't doing it to be cool so much as I was giving myself time to form a response. "I know where it is but we don't have it now. If you give me my mom, I'll take you to it."

"I don't trust you." She edged closer to me, her hand raised like she might slap me. Her eyes were almost black in the dark room. "Until you give me what I need, your mother will stay exactly where I left her."

My breath was coming in rapid bursts, and my heart started to pound. "I can't believe I thought you were nice. You're evil."

I balled up my fists, not knowing what to do with them. Rose's dad had gotten to his feet—the knee of his suit pants had ripped when he hit the ground and he was limping—and before she could stop him, he wrenched LaForge away from me.

"You really have his mother?" he said. He pushed

268

the hair from her face and sadly gazed into her eyes. "Chantal, you misled me to think that Owen had stolen something, but it's clear now that he's not the criminal here. If you have this boy's mother, you need to take him to her."

Rose seemed to let out a breath, as if she'd been worried her dad was part of the kidnapping plot. Now she understood for certain that he wasn't. But LaForge didn't answer Monsieur Bordage. Instead, she pulled something from the waistband of her jeans. It was the fireworks launcher she had used at the museum opening. She pointed it at me, like a gun. I gulped. Did it shoot bullets, too?

"Give me the real book, and no one will get hurt."

"I won't tell you where it is until you take me to my mother," I said. "Otherwise, you might as well shoot me. But then you'll never have Jules Verne's prophecy or the treasure it leads to."

LaForge said in a whisper, "The three of you don't know the first thing about Jules Verne. You think this is a game." She stepped closer to me with the launcher. I could tell she didn't want to fire it at me. She wanted the book.

"You have no idea what it's like to invest your life's work into something and still feel like no one will care the way you do. Do you know how many people will attend my exhibit?" A tear slipped from her eye. "The gala, yes, they come to the gala to see celebrities. But will they return to admire the years of work I put into the most comprehensive Jules Verne exhibit there's ever been? In my experience, likely not. Most people care more for the trivial than the important."

"Chantal, please stop. You are not thinking clearly and you will regret your actions," Mr. Bordage said.

"I'm sorry you think no one appreciates your work," I added. "But it doesn't mean you should hurt people."

"And yet I have your attention," she said. Her eyes were darting around. A chill pinballed through me. Something told me she wasn't going to say, "Oh you're excused," and let us leave.

I backed a few steps away, knocking into Rose and Nas, who caught me by the shoulders. "Maybe we should tell her about the thing," Nas said, and I knew he meant the desk.

"What thing?" LaForge said, an eager grin pulling up her lip.

Before I could decide what to do, a figure burst forward from behind a stack of crates. They were dressed in a hat, scarf, and trench coat.

"Stop, Chantal. Get away from them," bellowed a familiar voice. The scarf blew back from the person's face as they charged toward us.

It was Bessier.

I got between him and LaForge, poking him in the chest. "Are you in on this? Where's my mom?"

But he shoved me aside and reached for the launcher and LaForge. She yanked it out of his grasp but discharged the trigger. A small rocket, like the one at the museum party, shot out and into one of the crates.

Rose's dad, with a look of terror on his face, screamed at us. "Get down!" The box exploded into shards of wood and colorful gunpowder bursts. A flying board clocked him on the back, knocking him to the ground again.

His ankle was caught under a table that had fallen over. Rose started to rush toward him as more debris exploded into the air and came clattering to the floor. We rushed after her. We tried to lift the table off his leg but a number of boxes had toppled over and made the table impossible to maneuver.

"Even if you can move the table, you can't carry me," he told us. He reached a hand out to fondly touch Rose's face. "Please, I couldn't live with myself if something happened to you. You have to leave here now!"

"He's right," Nas said.

He and I stood and started toward the light from the open door. Rose looked caught between staying with her dad and going with us, but as more fireworks went off, the room filled with smoke and we couldn't see. She backed away from her father, coughing.

"Rose, come on!" I screamed to be heard over the dozens of explosions bursting right above us. "We can't stay here." We bent our heads and ran for the door.

"Where's Bessier?" Nas said.

"Or LaForge?" I said. I hated the lady, but without her, I had no chance of finding my mom.

There was no sign of them as we ran out toward the empty street. When we were a few steps onto the next block, an explosion louder than the one inside the factory shook the ground. The factory's high windows shattered and shards of glass rained from above, and a massive chunk of the brick wall fell inward with a deafening crash.

CHAPTER FORTY-ONE

Back to School

IT HAD ALL HAPPENED IN ABOUT FOUR SECONDS.

"Oh my god, my father," Rose said, clutching her stomach and stumbling like the building's continued shuddering was jolting her forward. "I shouldn't have left him."

I put an arm across her shoulders. "He told you to go," I said. "And, if something did happen to him, it would have happened to you, too." Rose half-nodded but she was staring into space, listening to the fire snap and crackle behind us. A huge sob racked her shoulders and she whispered to herself, "Why did I fight with him?"

I glanced at Nas, hoping he'd know what to say. But

before we could comfort Rose, a small car peeled around the corner and screeched to a stop in front of us. Bessier was in the driver's seat.

I backed away from the curb with an arm out to each side, protecting Nas and Rose behind me.

"You need to come with me," Bessier said. He pushed a button and the passenger door swung open.

"You work with LaForge," I spat. "No way."

"Chantal LaForge tried to kidnap me. She's no ally of mine," he said.

"He did try to take that fireworks gun from her, O," Nas said.

I stepped closer to Bessier's car as I peered up and down the street for signs of LaForge.

"If you're looking for her, she's long gone," Bessier said. "But she'll be searching for you, or one of her lackeys will. Get in."

We heard the unmistakable wail of police cars and fire trucks getting closer. "LaForge could have called them to trick us," Nas said. "Maybe we'd better go with Bessier."

I let Rose slide in first, and Nas and I squeezed in next to her in the small back seat. Rose leaned her head against the window, not talking to us, just watching the factory as it got smaller and smaller as we careened away.

"Where are you taking us?" I asked, because it

seemed like the thing you were supposed to ask, even if it wasn't like I had somewhere I wanted to go.

"You're not in any danger with me," Bessier said. It didn't answer my question and it was the kind of answer a bad guy would give if he wanted to buy your trust, but I didn't feel in danger with Bessier. He was weird, for sure, but I had no reason not to believe him.

Bessier zigzagged through the streets of Paris, which were dotted with couples and groups of friends out for the night. Nas pulled his phone from his pocket and tapped out a text. "Telling my parents I'm staying over with you," he said. "I just hope they don't ask to talk to your mom."

I started to recognize the landmarks around us and realized Bessier was heading toward the collège. When we got to the front of the building, he didn't park on the street. Instead, he made a sharp left turn down an alley alongside the school and pulled into a small underground parking area that must have been meant for the staff. Bessier got out and held a finger to his lips to indicate we should be quiet. The school building looked creepy, with pockets of light falling off into pools of darkness. I wondered if I was wrong to trust Bessier. I told myself that, at least if Bessier and LaForge had worked together to take my mom, I had one of them in my sights.

Nas and I got out of the car but Rose didn't seem to realize we'd stopped. She was still stuck in the same position, staring out the window.

Bessier turned in his seat and peered at her. "We can call the hospital from my office," Bessier said. He said everything slowly and very kindly. There was no trace of the stern teacher from class. "I called the paramedics and police before I picked you up. The emergency workers are sure to have found him."

Rose gulped back a sob. She moved to open the door of the car and climbed out weakly. Nas and I got on either side of her and put arms around her shoulders, helping her to stay steady on her feet.

As Bessier led us through the cavernous underground parking lot, he started to talk like he was teaching a class. Any other time, it would have been annoying, but right now it was calming, as if things weren't a complete mess.

"Jules Verne's works were so popular that he became one of the richest men in France," he began, walking in front of us, which, I thought, was not something someone who'd done you wrong would do. I could easily have clocked him in the back of the head.

"By the last year of his life, for some reason, he was out of money. He also burned many of his manuscripts, and no one understood why," he said. We'd come to a locked metal door. Bessier pulled a small key from his jacket and opened it, leading us into a narrow metal stairwell. We followed him up it, our steps rattling, then echoing. When we reached the top, he turned to face us, and the shadows flickered on his face.

"People assumed that he hid his riches, and a legend started to circulate that his treasure was somewhere in Paris. Many members of the Jules Verne Society joined more for that reason." He paused and rubbed his eyes. "I have nothing in common with those people. They're just out for riches. I always thought Jules Verne left us the real treasure right where we could find it. On the pages of his books. In the brilliant ideas he shared with us."

He unlocked the door at the top of the stairwell and pushed it open. We were inside his office. "Whoa," I said. The day had been awful, but it was hard not to be impressed with this secret passageway.

"I need a door like this," Nas said.

The room was still a mess but Bessier swept some broken items into his trash can and sat behind his desk. "I joined the society to preserve Jules Verne's legacy. Chantal LaForge did, too. We always felt irritated by people who wanted to learn about Jules Verne just to find the treasure. But over the years, we took different

278

paths. I know that not everyone will share my love of Jules Verne. I only hope with my classes students will come to appreciate his works."

He inhaled a long breath and slowly let it out. "Chantal LaForge is different. She's an expert like I am, and she is truly one of the only people I believe adores Jules Verne the way I do. But she wants the world to recognize her work. It's driven partly by her devotion to the author and partly by devotion to her ego. So, I made the mistake of telling her I thought someone had found a lost book and a key to his treasure. You see, I didn't believe Verne had hidden a treasure." Bessier looked at me. "I didn't believe…until I saw your book. *La Prophétie de Jules Verne*! A heretofore unknown work by one of the greatest science fiction writers of all time. The importance for scholarship was immeasurable! And I stupidly thought I would share it with another dedicated scholar."

I opened my mouth to tell him the book was gone and we only had a few pieces of random junk to show for it, but Bessier kept talking. "But I quickly changed my mind about Chantal. I worried she might want the book for her collections," he said. "Because I also believe— no, I know—that Jules Verne could see into the future, and he left nothing to chance. If you found the book, you were meant to. It wasn't my right to take it. So after

I called Chantal, I chose a decoy book instead, deciding I'd feign ignorance and let her think I was crazy. And that night when I hid the book there"—he pointed to the *Nautilus* with the secret compartment—"I knew you were watching, and I hid it so I could count on you finding it. I'm glad you figured out how to use my slippers." He handed me my Vans. I put them on because the Bête Noires were smelly from the Seine water. "I didn't count on the part where Chantal would send people to kidnap me. Oh, and I'll need my slippers back."

Now he pushed his old corded desk phone toward Rose. "You should use this to call the hospital, in case LaForge is tracking your phone."

Rose lifted the phone and pulled it as far as its cord would extend, to a corner of the office, so she got some privacy by ducking behind a life-size diver's suit.

"But if she kidnapped you," Nas said, "how did you get away? How do we know you're not actually working with her?"

Bessier smirked. "One good thing about reading so much Jules Verne is that I know how to get out of a scrape. And LaForge didn't hire the smartest goons. I told them I'd take them to the book and it would please their boss. Then I escaped."

Nas shot me a look and nodded, as if to say, "I believe him."

I believed him, too. "Then you decided to follow us?"

"I didn't follow you. I followed LaForge because I thought she was still up to no good. And, I found out tonight, I was right."

CHAPTER FORTY-TWO

An Unlikely Ally

IT MADE SENSE. PLUS, IT WAS HARD NOT TO BELIEVE BES-sier meant what he said, about wanting to preserve Jules Verne's legacy. Wasn't that what his whole office was about?

"I think you really do love Jules Verne, and I think his legacy matters to you," I said to Bessier. I glanced at Nas, then added, "We'd like your help."

Bessier smiled. The first smile I'd ever seen from him.

"There's only one problem," I said.

Bessier leaned across his desk, like he was about to tell me a secret. "And what's that?"

"I don't care about Jules Verne. I only want to save my mom...." I glanced toward Rose. "And make sure Rose's dad is okay, and no one else gets hurt."

Bessier stood up and crossed to the *Nautilus*. I gripped both arms of my chair, wondering if he was going to pull out a weapon or something. He ran a finger along the top of the *Nautilus* like it was a soft kitten. "I never imagined saying this, but I agree." He looked me in the eye as he said it, and I believed him. "Jules Verne would not have liked people getting hurt in his name."

Weirdly, even though Bessier seemed somewhat suspicious, I one hundred percent trusted that he was on our side. I was about to ask him what we should do next, when Rose yelped, with her hand covering the phone's mouthpiece. "He's okay! They brought my father in and he's being treated for light smoke inhalation and a sprained ankle."

Bessier clasped his hands like he was thanking someone and said to her, "Send him a message that you are okay via the nurse, but we cannot go to him. We need to figure out where LaForge is keeping Owen's mother first."

Rose started to speak again, doing as Bessier asked. When she hung up, I said to Bessier, "What do you know about LaForge? Where would she take my mom?"

Bessier came back to the desk and sat down, staring at the poster that said *Journey to Mars*. "I wish I could say," he told us. "But I can tell you this. LaForge will be desperate to get the book and whatever treasure it might lead to. She's also smart enough to know that you are closer to finding the treasure than she is. She won't hurt your mother—or you—if she thinks you'll lead her to it."

Hadn't he just said that my mom was more important than Jules Verne's dumb treasure? I stood up, glaring at him, and ready to say something, when Nas put a hand on my arm.

"So if we find the treasure, she'll find us, and bring Owen's mom," he said. The way Nas said it, I knew he was right. Meaning, Bessier was right.

284

Then my stomach plummeted. "But we don't have the book," I said.

"What happened to the book?" Bessier asked. Considering how excited he'd been about the book when I first brought it to class, he was surprisingly calm about it now that it was lost.

"There was this desk…at the big library…" I started to explain.

"It ate the book," Nas finished.

Bessier smirked. "Mr. Godfrey, Mr. Shirvani, that sounds like a new variation on 'the cat ate my homework' and yet, I believe you. So, without the book, what do we have?"

I pulled off my shoe and put the medallion on his desk. Rose and Nas pulled the crystal and the glasses from their hiding spots. "All we have is this stuff, and no idea how to use it."

Bessier spent what felt like an hour but was only a few minutes examining our items. The guy was really good at building suspense. Then he picked up the crystal.

"You don't have the book," he said. "But you have this, and I believe I know what it's for."

CHAPTER FORTY-THREE
An Un-Lazy Sunday

Sunday, June 21, 7:00 a.m.

BESSIER ENCOURAGED US ALL TO GET A BIT OF SLEEP
before we went on the next leg of our quest, and we were
so exhausted that no one argued. We helped him clean up
the dropped and broken Jules Verne memorabilia so we'd
have space to sleep. Early Sunday, I woke up and unfolded
myself from an uncomfortable position in Bessier's desk
chair and saw that he was already awake and had somehow gotten us a plate of chocolate croissants and coffee. I
trusted him even more, knowing that he could easily have
taken the crystal and medallion and locked us in here.

"Thanks for breakfast," I said to him. I didn't take my chances with coffee, after last time, but Rose poured herself a mug while Nas and I dug into the pastries.

When we'd finished eating, Bessier said we should walk, rather than take his car, to our next stop. "It will be safer, as I don't want LaForge tracking my car," he said.

The streets were still empty when we left the collège. It was seven o'clock on a Sunday morning, and the only sounds were birds and church bells. Bessier must have been a morning person because he was walking with a slight spring in his step. "How are we going to find the treasure without the book?" I asked him. "Won't it be impossible?"

"'All that is impossible remains to be accomplished,'" he said, and I knew it had to be a Jules Verne quote. "And, really, I'm not sure. But we'll start here."

We were in front of the Musée des Arts et Métiers. The hot-air balloon was still outside.

"You know, after the *Nautilus*, the invention most associated with Jules Verne is the hot-air balloon," he said, going into his lecture mode from class.

"I saw that movie *Around the World in Eighty Days*," Nas said. "I'd go by plane."

Bessier pointed at him. "Aha, but Jules Verne did not use a hot-air balloon in *Around the World in Eighty*

287

Days," he said. He watched the balloon outside the museum sway slightly as a breeze blew past. "There is one in his first book, *Five Weeks in a Balloon*. In *Around the World*, Jules Verne briefly brings up the balloon notion, in chapter thirty-two, but the characters dismiss it as highly risky."

Rose smiled. "But everyone mistakenly associates him with the balloons because of the old movie. My dad told me that, too."

Bessier patted her shoulder. "Your father is a smart man. And, to be fair, though I like the *Nautilus* submarine far more, hot-air balloons are quite a spectacle."

"It's definitely a good photo op," I said, admiring the balloon as it bobbed with the breeze. Something about Bessier continuing to drop Jules Verne knowledge even in a crisis made me feel hopeful. The guy was smart, and his attention to detail showed he really cared. He'd help us find my mom.

Nas had walked toward the museum door, but Bessier shook his head. "We're not going in there, and it's locked anyway," he said. He was walking toward the entry of a Métro station. "Come with me."

The station, like the street, was mostly empty, but the inside was instantly familiar.

"This looks like the room where the Jules Verne Society was having its secret party," I said. Like the room, the Métro station had a steampunk look, with curved bronze panels held together by oversized bolts. The only thing it didn't have were the booths and the bar. Instead, there were polished wood benches spaced along the tracks for people to sit on as they waited for the train.

And mixed in with the modern advertisements for cell phones and upcoming concerts were retro-looking posters, kind of like the ones in Bessier's office. A rocket ship, a cross-section of the earth, an undersea scene. Jules Verne-y stuff.

Bessier stopped at a poster with the *Nautilus* on it. He checked his watch and held up a finger, like he was telling us to wait a moment. About ten seconds later, a Métro train rumbled by without stopping. "Express train," Bessier said.

When the train's last car passed, he took a few steps to the next poster, which was a collage of Jules Verne imagery. A rocket, a hot-air balloon, and a submarine. The submarine was underwater, with a shark and an octopus swimming menacingly nearby. On the seafloor were various weird plants and shells, and one was a nautilus shell that looked exactly like the medallion. "May I have the medallion, Owen?" he asked. I handed it to him, and he took it, then pressed the design to the shell on the poster. It made a clicking noise.

The poster tilted inward, like a revolving door, but a vertical one. "As I suspected," Bessier said in a calm voice, as if he opened secret passages every day. Nas, Rose, and I watched in amazement as he bent his tall frame so he could squeeze beneath the opening. Then he peered out at us. "Come on," he said.

"Are you sure this is a good idea?" I asked.

"'It seems wisest to assume the worst from the beginning…and let anything better come as a surprise,'" Bessier said.

Rose tapped her chin. "Isn't that what the characters learn in *The Mysterious Island*?"

"Indeed."

"Is this a quest or an extra-credit assignment?" I asked, waiting for Rose as she crouched to enter the poster-door.

"This is for sure one of the most surreal weekends of my life," Nas said as he crawled in after her.

I followed him, thinking how easily Bessier might be leading us to some kind of tiny torture chamber. But, what choices did I really have, if I wanted to see my mom again?

As I passed through the small tunnel and unfolded myself on the other side, it all made sense.

"I've been here before," I said.

CHAPTER FORTY-FOUR

Everything Is Illuminated

WE WERE IN THE ROOM FROM THE PARTY. THE JULES Verne Society's secret room. It looked like the subway station, and vice versa, because they were connected. And, its attachment to the station also explained why the society's party had been interrupted by the rumbling noise. That had been a Métro train going by.

"Oh, thank goodness it's still here," Bessier said, walking toward the strange machine in the center of the room. It was bigger than I remembered it, but that might have been because this time it wasn't surrounded by people.

"That weird metal box?" Nas said. "What's it do?"

Bessier pointed to the engraved inscription. "'See the world through my eyes.'"

There was a small glass dome at the top of the machine. Bessier pushed the dome to the side and revealed a metal plate beneath it. At the center of the plate was an odd indentation, about the size of…

"The crystal," I said. I reached into a small pocket of the messenger bag and pulled out the velvet pouch from Deyrolle. I shook out the crystal inside and offered it to Bessier.

"No, you go ahead," he said, stepping aside. I lay the crystal into the indentation, turning it until its grooves matched up to the imprint. Bessier set the dome back on top of the crystal, and the machine churned to life with a hum.

As the gears shifted in the chamber below, a beam of light pulsed out, passing through the crystal and the clear dome, which began to spin. The beam spiraled wildly around at first, dancing across the design of Paris on the ceiling. Then, finally, it settled on a spot.

"It's near the Pont de l'Alma," Rose said.

"Yes, and that's where the treasure must be," Bessier noted. He put a hand on each of my shoulders and said, "You see, we'll find it and get your mother back."

A warm feeling washed over me as I imagined seeing my mom again, and how good it would feel to give her a hug. I closed my eyes for a second and heard the sound of someone clapping.

I opened my eyes. And the clapping was real.

It was coming from LaForge, who walked into the room from the museum entrance. Two big guys in black suits followed her, and between them they held on to my mom's arms.

"Mom!" I cried, ignoring LaForge's sneer. Seeing LaForge's goons holding her like that made my heart race and my breath stop in my chest. I took a long pump from my inhaler. My mom tried to take a step toward me but was held back by her escorts.

"Owen, are you okay?" she cried.

"I'm okay," I said. "I'm so glad to see you. We're going to fix this."

"Enough with the tender reunions," LaForge said, shooting my mom a cold glance. "As if you cared about your son, always leaving him alone day and night."

"You'd better watch what you say about me and my son," Mom said, in an angrier voice than I'd ever heard from her.

LaForge shook the comment off, like she couldn't be bothered. She strode into the room and tilted her head back, grinning at the point of light on the ceiling. "What wonderful work you've all done," she said to me, Rose, and Nas. She took a few more steps toward Bessier. "Even you. I suppose I should thank you."

Bessier flinched but stood taller. "Chantal, it didn't have to come to this," he said, not like a threat but more like he wished she could remember her old self. "You used to say recognition for scholarly pursuits didn't matter as much as acquiring wisdom."

LaForge, who only came up to his shoulder, rolled her eyes as he spoke.

"Yes, and so why would I not want wisdom only I can have? With the book, my life's work will have amounted to something. I'll be the foremost expert on Jules Verne, because I'll be the only one to have read his prophecy."

"These smart kids have read it. Before you did," Bessier said. "And they no longer have it."

Why was he telling her that? If we couldn't turn over the book, we couldn't make the trade.

LaForge shrugged. "Then I suppose the boy no longer has a mother and his mother can no longer be reunited with him," she said. She nodded toward the goons, who were taking my mom toward the door to the Métro station. As one held the door up, the other shoved my mom through. As my mom crawled underneath, she peered back at me and called out, "Owen, be careful."

I tried to run toward her but the second goon pushed my chest with his meaty palm and I fell to the floor.

"I'll get the book back for you, if you give me my mom," I said, scrambling to my feet. LaForge was watching me like she found my distress amusing. I didn't care. I clasped my hands together and begged. "I know where it is."

LaForge smiled at me, almost kindly. "Well, the book is obviously only one of the treasures. It seems there's more to be discovered? The Pont de l'Alma, non? Imagine what a story it will be when the curator of the Arts et Métiers Jules Verne exhibit uncovers this huge find—who knows what he hid?"

"Then why must you take the boy's mother?" Bessier asked, stepping closer to LaForge, who took a step backward toward the secret door.

"I'm a curator," she said. "I know the value of insurance."

Before we could do anything, LaForge kicked the door with the heel of her boot and ducked elegantly beneath it as it swung upward. Bessier's eyes almost popped out of his head as he realized she was escaping. He lunged for the door as it began to close.

"Adieu!" LaForge called. She tossed a small metal ball at Bessier's chest, and it exploded into a cloud of gray ash.

Particles of whatever it was went up my nose and I started to sneeze uncontrollably. We all did. The dust was finely ground pepper, like the kind my mom put on cacio e pepe. Every time I sneezed, more of it got into my nostrils and my mouth.

As the cloud began to clear and my sneezing subsided, I jumped off with both feet, trying to hurl myself at the door LaForge had exited. But I hit the wall as the opening clicked shut and a very final metallic clunk came from the other side. I pushed on it but it wouldn't move. LaForge and the goons must have blocked it with something.

Then I heard the sound of a train.

"There won't be another train for at least twelve minutes," Bessier said sadly. "But we know where they're going."

CHAPTER FORTY-FIVE

Up in the Air

Sunday, June 21, 8:45 a.m.

I SHOULD HAVE BEEN MORE DEPRESSED THAT WE'D LET LaForge get away, but here was the thing: I'd seen my mom, and knowing that she was okay gave me some kind of inner strength, because all at once, I knew I'd get to her at any cost.

That was, until we left the museum. My plan—to hail a taxi—was instantly out because the streets were no longer empty. Now it seemed like every person in Paris had started their Sunday errands, and the street was jammed with traffic.

"We'll never catch up to them," Rose said, waving at taxis that already had riders. "The roads are so full."

The sun was shining right on the rainbow stripes of the hot-air balloon. I sneezed a few more times, from the pepper, and as I did, an idea blazed into my brain. A very brilliant idea.

"'Roads? Where we're going, we don't need roads,'" I said.

"Are you quoting Jules Verne now, too?" Nas said.

"Nah," I said. "Doc Brown from *Back to the Future*. It's a movie from the eighties I watched with my mom."

I raced over to the hot-air balloon, checking out the basket and the ropes that were holding it to the ground.

Bessier cleared his throat. "Owen, I hope you're not thinking what I think you're thinking."

"If it's that we should take this balloon and beat LaForge to the next spot, then you nailed it."

Bessier shook his head. "Did you not hear me? What Jules Verne himself said about hot-air balloons? Highly risky! Impossible!"

I shrugged. "But then later you said, 'All that is impossible remains to be accomplished.'"

Bessier's lip twitched up. He grimaced and looked up at the balloon, like he was wondering if it actually worked. I was wondering the same thing.

"It will weigh too much with all of us." I wondered

if he was afraid of heights like Nas, but now wasn't the time to get into Bessier's phobias.

"Are you with me?" I asked Rose and Nas.

"We have been this far," Nas said. His eyes were watery from LaForge's pepper bomb. He seemed about as excited about the balloon idea as a snail would be to go on a pizza. "Are you sure we have to take this thing?"

"You can wait with Bessier," I said to him.

Nas glanced at our teacher, whose arm was waving uselessly in the air as cabs passed him by. "Fine, I'm coming," Nas said. "Only because you might need me."

"Of course we will," Rose said. Then she paused. "We still don't have an exact location. We just know the light shone somewhere near the Alma bridge. I worry we need the book to know exactly where to go. For the treasure. And Owen's mom."

Mom… The first thing I'd do would be to apologize for ripping up my paper, and the chaos that one action had caused. She'd like that. But how would I ever apologize if I didn't find her? Rose was right. We needed the book. Hold on… The book I'd also ripped.

"Wait…," I said. I reached into my pocket and pulled out the ripped pages I'd torn from the book the day before. I flattened them out on a bench outside the museum. I'd always been pretty good at puzzles, so it didn't take long to reassemble the pages. Still, it was a long shot to think the pages I had torn from the book were somehow going to be the ones we needed.

It was a drawing of a man, holding up a rock, flanked on either side by two sea serpent creatures. "If this is a clue, I don't get it," Rose said.

Nas tilted his head, looking at it from a different angle. "It seems familiar, though," he said.

It did. And then I thought back to the day my back-pack had been stolen. How at Le Dôme, just before I saw the kid running away with my stuff, I'd been staring at the sculpture at the center of the frieze, and the kid had rushed down the stairs and jumped over one of the sea serpents.

I squinted at the page. Along the tail of one of the sea serpents, in tiny letters, were the words, *See the world through my eyes*.

"That's from Le Dôme! And it's the same thing the machine says," Nas said, looking proud to have figured it out.

"You're a genius," I told him. And so was Bessier. He'd said that if the book wound up in my hands, it was as Jules Verne intended. And now the book was leading me back to where this had all begun. It made so much sense, it didn't make sense.

"Let's go," I called to my friends. I started to climb

in the basket attached to the balloon. "Looks like we're taking this to Le Dôme."

"Are you sure about this?" Bessier said, wandering over from his spot near the curb.

"You said yourself that I found the book for a reason," I reminded him. "Maybe there's also a reason there happens to be a hot-air balloon right here when I most need transportation."

"We could wait for the Métro," Rose said. "It won't be that long."

"And it could get delayed on the tracks," I said. "Nope. Do me a favor and yank up one of those stakes as you get in."

Rose tugged the rope tied to the stake and then one side of the basket seemed to float ever so slightly off the ground.

Nas got in on the other side and pulled up the remaining stake. Now we were a few feet off the ground. "Hmm. I don't think this is working," Nas said.

I was studying a small lever attached to a tank beneath the opening of the balloon. A cautionary sticker of a flame was on it. "It's a hot-air balloon, so it needs hot air." I flipped the lever down and fire spouted out from the tank. The balloon was rising! Fast.

Nas grabbed his stomach. "I don't think you want to see that croissant I ate, Owen, so go easy."

302

As the balloon lifted off the ground, people on the sidewalk stopped and stared. Drivers even slammed on their brakes. A guy on a scooter drove up onto the median as he watched us lift off. Bessier seemed to forget he needed a taxi as he turned to watch us with a look of amazement. We cleared the pointed top of the Musée des Arts et Métiers and drifted over an apartment building. A woman in a robe sipping coffee on the rooftop smiled and waved at us, then—as if realizing it was not normal to see three kids flying a hot-air balloon—did a double take and nearly fumbled her coffee.

We waved at her. "Bonjour!" Rose called. Then she turned to me. "I can't believe you got it off the ground," Rose said. "But what now?"

We were high above the city, cresting the tops of buildings and being carried by a wind that was blowing west. "I think it's all wind," I said. "We just have to pick up the right current to take us in the right direction."

Nas was gripping the side of the basket. "How do you know all this?"

I shrugged. "Video games, I guess," I said. "Okay, Le Dôme is that way. I think."

Rose pointed to the Seine below. "Follow the river's path. It leads to Le Dôme."

The wind was already carrying us that way but slowly, so I twisted the propane valve again, thinking more heat

303

might get us there faster. We lifted higher into the air, where the wind was coming in more urgent gusts. The basket bumped and rattled as the currents lifted us.

I thought we were doing really well but then I must have accidentally turned the valve the wrong way, bringing the propane flame too low just as a current of wind grabbed hold of the balloon. In an instant, we tore across the sky. In the *wrong* direction.

I kicked up the flame a few notches, but I'd lost some control of the balloon.

"Owen...," Nas said, his voice barely audible. "Owen." He grabbed my shoulder and turned me around. "What should we do about that?"

The Eiffel Tower! We were coasting right at it.

I had to get us higher again, back into the counter-current above us. But the wave of wind we were riding on picked up speed. I couldn't change course.

"You need to get us down. As fast as possible," Rose said. "If we hit the tower..."

"We can't land here. We're too far from Le Dôme," I said. I didn't mention that there was nowhere to land. The city around the Eiffel Tower was crowded with people and cars and zero open space. "We won't hit the tower," I promised.

And then we hit the tower.

Our basket smacked against the window of the

restaurant on the Eiffel Tower's second floor. The people eating inside stopped with their food halfway to their mouths and stared at us.

A kid actually glanced up from his iPhone and I could read his lips as he said, "Holy crap!"

"Owen, we're heading for the observation deck, and this is not the way you should see the Eiffel Tower for the first time."

Rose was right. The balloon was rising along the side of the Eiffel Tower. Besides taking us in the wrong direction, it also meant we might hit the pointy top of the tower. Balloons and pointy things were not a good combo.

Maybe it was the panic, but I instantly knew what to do to get us out of trouble. I ratcheted up the valve, giving the propane flame a nice little burst. The balloon, which had been hugging the edge of the tower and slowly bobbing up, shot straight into the air.

We were rocketing toward the top of the Eiffel Tower and I couldn't decide if it would be better to get deflated by the spire or blast into space. Those seemed like our only two options.

"This! Is! Bad!" I said.

"Can you lower us? Turn down the heat?" Rose said. Her knuckles shone white as she gripped the side of the balloon basket.

We had hurtled above the Eiffel Tower and were rising way too quickly for it to be good. Below us, I could see the entire city of Paris, maybe even better than I could have from the top of the tower. If this had been a tourist excursion, it would be awesome, but the farther off the ground we were, the less likely I'd be to land us where we needed to be.

I cranked the valve to lower the heat. It felt like going over the tallest hill on the Metal Dragon, my favorite roller coaster. My stomach completely detached from inside of me and I was surprised not to see my own guts floating on air. "Nooooo," Nas wailed as we plunged from the sky.

Then...

HIISSSSSSSSSSSSSSSSSSSSSSSSSSSSSS.

The balloon had caught on the Eiffel Tower! We were leaking air!

People in the observation deck screamed and started clattering toward the exits. A security guard waved his baton at us and yelled, "Get down from there, right now!" in French. Actually, he might have said something much nastier. I didn't have time to translate.

"We'd love that," Rose said back, in French. "Do you have any ideas?"

The guard glared at her as his coworkers came to

back him up by also shaking batons at us. It was not super effective.

"Any?" I asked Rose and Nas as calmly as I could.

Nas gulped. "Remember how I said I was afraid of heights? That's definitely truer than ever."

"Just close your eyes," Rose said.

"Okay, and forget that I am sitting in a basket one billion feet off the ground? No problem," Nas said. He sank down to the bottom of the balloon and held his head in his hands.

A big gust of wind ripped through the tower's metal frame and shook the basket. Rose lost her grip on the basket and tripped toward me. I reached out and caught her before she landed on Nas.

She glanced up at me and smiled. The wind had blown her hair everywhere, but she looked really pretty. "Thank you," she said.

"Anytime," I said, not thinking how it was very possible we were all going to die and my "anytime" would be the only time.

From his curled-in-a-ball position, Nas moaned. Another gust of wind made the basket sway even farther away from the tower, so we were almost horizontal with the ground.

"I hate this!" Nas said.

And then, we were free! The wind must have dislodged the bit of the balloon that had been caught. The balloon kept spitting air from the hole in the canvas, but it was intact enough to stay in the air.

We were floating again!

HISSSSSSSSSSSSSSSSSSSSS!

Air kept escaping…

My stomach dropped as the balloon plummeted. We were falling…

Fast!

I cranked the heat, trying to give the leaking balloon

as much lift as possible. I used every bit of the propane to heat the balloon's air enough to lift us into the current above us, which was blowing us back in the direction of Le Dôme. The heat from the flame warmed my cheeks as we propelled upward and into the current. I could do this! I had us sailing again! This was not impossible, like Bessier had said. Or at least it wasn't impossible for me.

The ride was bumpy and we were skidding across the sky, but we would make it to Le Dôme. I turned the propane up to the maximum level, trying to ignore the sound of air as it leaked from our punctured balloon.

"We're almost there," I said to my friends. And to the balloon, which seemed like it could use a pep talk.

Rose grabbed my shoulder excitedly and pointed. "I see it! We're going to make it!"

But then, the flame from the propane tank suddenly sputtered to nothing, and we started to sink.

"No, no, no, no, we don't want to land yet," I said, I guess to the balloon again. The high altitude was making me think it could hear me. "Please just hang on a little longer."

"I'm trying, O," Nas croaked, with his eyes scrunched closed. The wind shifted, and a cross breeze knocked us in the other direction. The gust hit the basket so hard, it tipped to the side like we'd been swatted by a giant. Somehow, we stayed in the basket. It was a miracle.

I whacked the propane tank with the side of my hand, and a flame reappeared. It wasn't going to be enough for a smooth ride; we were bumping toward Le Dôme as the balloon started to deflate. The wind gusted against the sagging balloon, causing the canvas to flap angrily.

"We have to land this thing," Rose said. "Le Dôme is over there, but maybe we just land close to it, here?" She pointed to the street below. But I didn't want to lose any more time. Or get hit by a car.

I saw a cord that led up to the top of the balloon. Maybe it let air out or something.

"Do you remember anything from *Five Weeks in a Balloon*?" I asked Rose. "Or what that does?" I pointed to the cord.

"It was the first Jules Verne my dad read me. I was five!" she said.

"Okay, then," I said, and I pulled the cord. Air shot out from the top of the balloon as we dropped lower and lower, catching a gust of air that dragged us along with the drooping balloon out front like a sail, and our basket trailing behind it at a dangerous angle.

We were going in the direction of Le Dôme but so fast that we'd overshoot it.

310

I cut the heat even more, so we deflated faster.

We dropped swiftly and my knees went wavy. We were rattling along fast, as the balloon started to sink around us. "We'll be there in no time."

"Or dead even sooner," Nas said.

"Just tuck and roll if you have to!" I yelled over the balloon's loud whining, as I saw where we were about to land.

SPLASH!

The basket plummeted into the green water of Le Dôme's fountain. The impact sent the gnarly-looking water sloshing over the edges of the pool. People who'd been sitting along the sides of the fountain screamed and scattered. The water wasn't deep but it seeped in the sides of the basket, soaking us to our knees.

A discarded cigarette package and a slimy brown leaf stuck to my shin. I looked around, barely believing we'd made it.

Several of the skaters stopped mid-trick to stare at us and take videos on their phones.

One guy started to clap.

"Act normal," Rose said, stepping lightly out of the basket and neatly hopping to the edge of the fountain.

I gave the videographers a little bow. Rose rolled her eyes.

Nas wobbled out, then sprinted for a trash can,

311

where he did what he'd been waiting to do since we took off. But no one noticed because there was a hot-air balloon deflating in the fountain.

"Okay, so we made it," I said, walking toward the part of the frieze with the guy corralling sea serpents. The same one that was on the page I'd torn from the book. "Now, how do I see the world through Jules Verne's eyes?"

CHAPTER FORTY-SIX

The Final Destination?

I TOOK OUT THE CRYSTAL AGAIN, BECAUSE IT HAD WORKED before, and held it up to my eye, peering through it at the sea serpent man and the rest of the frieze. Nothing. "Wait, the glasses," I said. I scrambled to get them out, knowing we had to move fast. We'd just landed a stolen hot-air balloon in the fountain at Le Dôme. Someone was going to want to talk to us.

"Weren't you listening?" Nas said. "Those glasses are garbage. You can't see anything through them."

If I could fly a balloon, I could figure out how to

work some weird glasses. I ignored Nas and slipped them on. They were really wide and I had to hold them against my temples, but right away, I could see they were trying to show me something. Beams of light filtered in and started to rearrange. As I turned my head from side to side, the beams joined together into one bright yellow arrow of light that sorted itself like pixels on a screen. It formed a line that led away from my nose, then revolved, landing in a pattern. On the frieze.

The light had made itself into a shape on top of the frieze. It zigzagged and turned through the carved figures. "It's a map! I think!" I dashed over to a kid drawing in a sketchbook and said, "Can I borrow that?"

The kid gave me his pad and pencil. I thanked him and started to sketch the extra details that became apparent when you looked through the glasses.

Woven between the sculptures built into the frieze was a path.

It started where we were standing, and with arrows, pointed in the direction of the Seine.

It stopped with a drawing of a rectangle underneath an upside-down U.

"What's that mean?"

"Maybe it's another code for something?" Rose said. "Or Morse code?"

"Or another symbol cut in half?" Nas said.

I thought of something my mom said a lot, that sometimes the simplest answer was the right one. "What if it's just a door under a bridge?"

"It's a good time to go hide under a bridge," Nas said. "Because the cops are here again."

Officer Sadface and his pals were stepping around the hot-air balloon. We took off running, toward the Alma bridge. Instead of crossing it, we ran onto the path along the Seine that went beneath it. "The door," Rose said, stopping at a giant brass door with a big wheel in its center, like a bank vault's. I cranked the wheel and heard something catch inside, metal on metal. The door opened with a pop, like I'd pulled a giant suction cup off a window. There were stairs inside, and we took them down, down, down. The walls around us were coated in a green moss, and the air smelled like wet dog.

We were standing on a small platform with a power box and a bucket and mop. But it was a dead end.

I checked the map I'd drawn. "This seems like the right place."

"But there's nothing here," Nas said.

"Look for a door or something," Rose said. She started pushing on the walls and Nas began knocking in search of something hollow that would open.

"I don't know," I said. I opened the power box, wondering if the treasure was in there. But when I opened it, all I saw were regular old switches, like the fuse box at home. My heart sank. I didn't know where my mom was, we'd lost the book, and I had no idea where else the path from Le Dôme could lead. "Maybe we have to go back to the frieze. I think I drew this wrong, because it says from here we go down. But I don't see an elevator."

Rose must have heard the shakiness in my voice because she patted my shoulder. "We'll figure it out," she said.

Nas chucked me on the shoulder. "Yeah, O," he added. "It's gonna be all right." I stared at the fuses, most of which had labels with names of streets written next to them. They were probably for traffic lights. The labels were yellowed and old. They were probably all computerized now. But even traffic lights wouldn't have been around until after Jules Verne's time. So he wouldn't have been down here. We were in the wrong place.

I started to close the cover to the power box. But then a switch that looked a little different from the others caught my eye. It was made of brass and greened with age where the others were made of black metal. But it was the label next to it that caught my eye. The handwriting was tiny and sort of familiar. CENTRE DE LA TERRE—NE TOUCHEZ PAS ET JOUISSEZ-EN!

I translated it slowly. "Center of the Earth...Do Not Touch and..." I paused. "What does Jouissez mean again?"

"Enjoy," Rose said. She and Nas crowded around me, reading the label over my shoulder.

"Don't touch, and enjoy? That makes no sense," Nas said.

"It makes perfect sense if you're an explorer who seeks adventure no matter the risk. It makes Jules Verne sense," I said. I looked at my friends. "Are you ready?"

"I don't really have a choice," Nas said. Rose nodded.

I held the switch between my thumb and my index finger and closed my eyes. I made a wish that this was going to work. Slowly, I moved the rusty switch from left to right. It made a metallic click that echoed.

I opened my eyes, hoping to see a secret door. Rose and Nas were looking around, too.

"Maybe you're not supposed to touch that one because it doesn't do anything?" she said.

"The map led us here and there's a switch named after a Jules Verne book! How could this not be the place?" I stomped my foot angrily on the ground.

And suddenly the chamber we were in started to lower itself like an elevator.

The walls stretched above us. The chamber around us was made of gray brick and the farther down we got, the stronger the mildew smell. Then the brick walls changed to metal, and finally, we stopped moving.

I spun around and saw a door cut into the metal. I pushed on it and couldn't get it to budge. "It's rusted shut," I said. "Help me push!"

The three of us started banging our shoulders against the door and kicking the bottom of it, sending chips of green paint and rust into the air around us. The chamber was getting hot and I started to feel claustrophobic. What if we were trapped down here?

"Stand back," Rose said to me and Nas. We moved to the side and watched as Rose stared at the door like a bullfighter. Then she got into a pose with one foot behind the other and stomp-kicked with her back leg, hitting the door square in the middle with her heavy combat boot.

It popped open. Nas and I exchanged a "Whoa" look.

"Are you a black belt or something?" I asked Rose.

"No, but seven years of ballet plus a brother who makes me watch pro wrestling. I learned a few things."

We stepped out into a huge limestone room with a high stone ceiling.

The space around us had stone floors and was big enough to store a plane—or at least the size of two basketball courts but with a seam running between them. Above us were massive copper pipes, each wide enough to fit a person inside. They curved along the domed ceiling, and several of them were open at one end, like giant faucets. Fat droplets of water plopped down from the open pipes and trickled across the stone floor, until they funneled into the pocket of the seam. At the far end of the room the stone floor gave way to a pool of water deep enough that I couldn't tell where the bottom was. Its surface was still, so it almost looked like dark gray glass.

"Where are we?" Nas asked.

"I think we're under the Seine," Rose said. "How did he know about this place?"

"I'm not sure, but I think he built it, to hide that," I said. I pointed across the room. On a platform made of stone that blended in with the wall behind it was a gray metal box about the size of a small carry-on bag.

"That has to be the treasure," Nas said.

"I almost can't believe it's real!" I said. We ran across the floor. All we needed to do was open the box, take the treasure, and find LaForge again. We'd make the trade and I'd have my mom back.

The metal was cool and a little damp on the outside. I put my hands on either side of the lid and tried to lift it. It was locked.

"Oh no, what if we were supposed to find some kind of key," Nas said.

"Look at this," Rose said, pointing to a small engraving of a nautilus symbol. The top half of it was on the box's lid and its bottom half was on the box itself.

"Finally, an easy one," I said.

I pulled the medallion from under my T-shirt and pressed its nautilus symbol to the one on the chest. It clicked into place and the box's lid popped open.

At first, we just stared at each other, like we were worried if we looked inside there'd be nothing there.

"I have to see this," Nas said. He peered inside.

"Incredible." He lifted out a sheaf of paper, bound on one side with string. "Looks like a manuscript."

I turned toward the box and took a look. It was filled with handwritten pages. I carefully lifted one of the yellowing sheaves of paper. A title page called it *A Quest Through Time*, and Jules Verne's signature was along the bottom. I flipped through it and saw more of Jules Verne's handwriting in the margins, like he'd been making notes for a revision. "Bessier is going to freak."

Rose took out the next one. She smiled as she flipped through the pages. "I think this one might be a romance novel. By Jules Verne."

I let out a deep breath. "I can't believe we found all this," I said. "Can you imagine what Jules Verne's fans are going to think when they hear about this?"

"This treasure is HUGE," Rose said.

CHAPTER FORTY-SEVEN

Twenty Thousand Leagues Under the Seine, Maybe

Sunday, June 21, 11:56 a.m.

"Owen! Are you okay?" I heard my mom's voice behind us and spun around.

"Mom!" My voice caught. Because the first face I saw was LaForge's. She was standing on the landing just inside the underground cavern, with Mom behind her. The goons were still clutching Mom's shoulders.

"When we got to Pont de l'Alma, we couldn't figure out what to do next, but I knew if we waited and followed you, we'd find out!" LaForge's eyes were gleaming with excitement. My grip tightened on the manuscript as LaForge walked toward us, her goons and my mom behind her. My mom twisted angrily against their grips, but they didn't let go. Finally, Mom heaved a sigh. "Owen, you didn't answer. Are you okay?" she said.

"I'm fine," I said. "But are you okay?"

"Yes, Owen. Just don't give her those manuscripts," she said.

"Oh please," LaForge said. "As if he cares about a bunch of old books. You just want your mommy, don't you?" She smirked as she shoved her way between me and Rose to see what was in the box.

I felt myself turn red because the truth was, I did want my mommy, even if it was embarrassing to have LaForge say that in front of my friends.

"Fine," I said. I thrust the book I was holding at LaForge. "Take it."

"Take them all," Rose said, dropping the manuscript she was holding back into the box. As she did, she caught my eye and put her palm on her chest, just below her throat. She widened her eyes. I knew she meant to keep the medallion for ourselves, and I gave her a small nod.

"Yep. It's all yours," I said. "Nas, give her the manuscript."

Nas huffed an irritated breath and handed LaForge the book he was holding. "Can't believe I thought you were cool." LaForge ignored us all as she greedily flipped through the sheaves of paper. Then she turned toward the chest and lifted out all the remaining manuscripts. She hugged them to her.

"You're welcome," Rose said sarcastically. "And now do we get Owen's mom back?"

LaForge glared at Rose. "I'm not going to miss you," she said. She spun away from us and snapped her fingers in the direction of the goons, who let go of my mom.

Once she was free, my mom wrapped me in a huge hug, and then opened her arms again so that Rose and Nas could join in. "You made some very good friends," she said.

While we were hugging, LaForge had scampered back across the cavernous space to her helpers. "Well," she said. "I'm so glad this worked out for everyone!" She sounded like a mom who'd hosted a successful playdate. I was trying to think of a snappy comeback, but before I could, LaForge tucked the manuscripts into a black leather bag and took off.

She and the goons hurried back up the elevator. We stepped out of our hug and my mom turned to me. "So, we need to talk about the balloon, Owen."

"Um, don't I get credit for rescuing you?" I said. "And finding this treasure, even if we did have to give it to LaForge?" Just to be sure, I peeked inside the chest one more time, hoping LaForge had missed something. But it was empty. The important thing was, I had my mom. And technically, we still knew the location of the prophecy book, even if we didn't know how to get it out of that desk. I shut the box's lid and turned back toward my mom and my friends.

"So, does this mean you can finally take a day off work?"

"I think a week at least," she said. "You can have that sleepover you asked for."

Rose tapped my shoulder and Nas cleared his throat.

"You might want to see this, Owen," he said.

A small door had opened in the stone wall, and the metal box was sliding backward on its platform. It fit neatly into a rectangular space, and the door slid closed, covering it.

I didn't know exactly what was happening, but I had a bad feeling about it. "We gotta get out of here," I said. We ran toward the elevator but it wasn't there. I flipped a switch on the wall but it did nothing. LaForge must have disabled it up above.

Over our heads, the pipes groaned like an overpopulated haunted house. Then:

CLANNNNGGGG! CREEEEEAAAAAKKK!

A deep, bellowing noise like a thousand toilets flushing at once sounded from above, and all at once, the giant pipes began to spew water into the room. A gush of water hit me and knocked me to the floor. I was on my knees, trying to stand back up when the ground started to shake. I skidded toward the seam in the floor just as it started to open.

My mom ran toward me and grabbed my arm, yanking me away just as the floor completely opened up and water started shooting in from beneath us, too. We went under and my mom let go of me and pointed up. We surfaced, spitting out nasty gray water.

Rose and Nas were a few feet away. Rose was treading water and telling Nas how to do it. "Just stay calm and keep your feet moving," she was saying. "Grab on to my shoulder if you need to." My mom and I dog-paddled toward them. The water kept pouring from above. I had no idea how deep this was.

"I can barely tread water," Nas said. "This is embarrassing, but I just started swim lessons."

The water level was rising, pushing us all up closer to the ceiling. "If the water doesn't stop, we're going to drown," Rose said. She was bobbing toward one of the overhead waterfalls and its stream hit her, sending her below the surface.

"Rose!" I said. I swam toward her and got hold of her arm, pulling her back up. She emerged from under the water and choked out a thank-you. She pushed her wet hair out of her face. She might have been crying but I couldn't be sure since we were all soaked.

"It's so deep," she said. "You can't see anything, and I don't know how far down we'd have to go to even come out in the Seine."

I'd finally saved my mom and now we were all going to die.

The space between us and the ceiling was getting even smaller. "Diving down and swimming is our only option," I said. "We're trapped, but maybe we can find a way out and into the Seine and to the surface."

"There's no way we can make it." Nas gulped, trying to keep his head above the surface.

"He's right," my mom said. "We don't know how deep it is or even if there's a way out." I was starting to get tired from treading,

"What…do…we…do…," I said to Rose. She looked at me and was about to say something, but then reached her arm out from the water and pointed at me. "You're glowing." She was pointing at my shirt, which was stuck to my skin. But beneath the fabric and the water was a faint green light.

"The medallion!" I yanked it out from under my

shirt. It was pulsing green. It was beeping, too. "What is it doing?"

The water underneath us turned a glowing green, just like the medallion. Waves churned and the water bubbled and the green light got closer and closer to us.

"I don't think I like this," Rose said, her face illuminated by the approaching light.

All of a sudden, I realized.

"I know what this is."

I started to recite a familiar passage.

"'The monster emerged some fathoms from the water, and then threw out that very intense but mysterious light mentioned in the report of several captains. This magnificent irradiation must have been produced by an agent of great shining power.'"

But then, my breath ran out. I tried to catch it, but just swallowed water. I gasped. And then…oatmeal.

I was having an asthma attack.

And I was drowning.

As my head sank below the water, I could hear my mom screaming, "Owen!"

I tried to kick and paddle, but it was no use, I was losing strength and sinking.

But then, my feet touched something solid. I was standing on something. It started to rise up through the water.

"Put your feet down, guys," I managed to say between gasps, as soon as my head was back above water. The water around us began to churn with tons of tiny bubbles. The green light got brighter and brighter, bathing the whole chamber in its glow as suddenly a bronze-and-glass dome peeked out from the foam.

My mom made it over to me and handed me an inhaler. She always carried one of my spares. I took a drag on it and my lungs opened.

My head was above water and I could breathe. We were all okay. Nas had his eyes closed—he must have been preparing for the worst—but he slowly opened them.

We all stared at each other. Because now we were standing on a deck.

And from the deck extended an immense, elongated metal oval.

We were standing on a submarine.

And not just any submarine.

Jules Verne's treasure was the *Nautilus*.

And it had come to pick us up.

CHAPTER FORTY-EIGHT

Just, Whoa

THE GLOWING WATER STARTED TO CHURN AND BUBBLE even more wildly. The pipes above us mercifully stopped pouring, and a whooshing noise filled the cavern as the vessel's top half bobbed to the water's surface.

The *Nautilus*, which I'd summoned with the medallion. It was about fifty thousand times cooler than a self-driving car.

We were drenched and standing on the deck, with our heads very close to touching the pipes on the ceiling. All four of us were trying to catch our breath.

"I thought we were gonna die," Nas said. "Or at least me."

"We wouldn't let you die," I said.

"How on earth did this get here?" my mom said. "What was that light? And that necklace?"

"It's a long story," Rose said. She put her arm around my mom. I walked toward the far end of the ship, to the domed part. As I got near it, something beeped and a round hatch beneath the dome slowly rose open.

"Should we get in?" Nas asked.

I looked at him. "I think this is definitely better than swimming."

Rose was leading my mom toward the hatch. "Dr. Godfrey, come on," she said. I saw my mom smile. She loved when people remembered to call her "doctor." Nas and I stepped back, so they could get in first.

Nas and I climbed in behind them, and in the shortest amount of time possible, I tried to take in the sheer awesomeness of being inside Jules Verne's greatest creation. The inside of the sub seemed brand-new. Beneath the hatch was a spiral staircase that led down to a control room with gears, gauges, and knobs, and a steering column, like in a plane. The seats were creamy butter-colored leather, and we all stopped to look at them. The leather was embossed with the nautilus shell design from the medallion, and a letter *N* in script above it. I ran my fingers over it, wondering why Jules Verne hadn't put his initials there.

"Who's driving?" Nas said, breaking into my thoughts. "Because I don't know what any of that stuff does."

I had the weirdest sense of déjà vu, and I plopped down behind the steering column. "Maybe I'll go two for two on working rare modes of transportation."

Rose poked me. "Maybe is dangerous."

"Okay, okay," I said. I flipped a switch that conveniently said DÉMARRER (which means "start" in French) and the sub churned to life with a rumble. Right away, I could feel the water cascading above and below us, almost like when the ocean rolls out under your feet.

I pulled down the lever and the top of the sub closed above us. We started to sink beneath the water. "Whoa, that's rad," Nas said. "Also, please don't let us drown."

"I got this," I said, sounding more confident than I felt.

Mom was studying the control panels and buttons and murmured, "This technology is amazing. This sub has to date back to the late 1800s, at least, but it looks so modern."

I pressed a button labeled CARTE (French for "map")

that showed the walls around us and a path ahead. A dot blinked in a narrow space. "That must be us, the *Nautilus*, where we are now." Farther along, the narrow path opened wider. "And that must be the Seine."

I pulled back on the handles and we lurched forward in a way that made my stomach feel like I'd left it behind. Then we plunged down, below the surface of the water.

The room we'd been in must have been some kind of underwater dock. Through the window, we saw the floor of the room where it had separated. We sank lower and lower, and finally we were at the very bottom of what must have been the river.

I pulled back on the steering handles and we burst forward. I let up a little so we were gliding more. I instinctively knew what to do, just like I had with the balloon. But the other weird thing was that the *Nautilus* had to be at least twenty feet long but it felt as easy to drive as the *Mario Kart* machine at my favorite arcade in Connecticut.

As we turned into the wider channel of the Seine, light from above shone down through the water. Fish swam in front of the windows. Mixed in with the grasses and mud at the bottom of the river was a lot of garbage. Someone's rusty old bike. A lot of McDo containers. A spooky baby doll with one eye.

333

"As cool as it is driving this thing, I could really use some food," I said.

"I'm starving," Rose agreed.

My mom nodded. "Surprisingly, the food when you're kidnapped isn't very good."

"And I really would like to change my clothes," Nas added.

"No problem," I said, and guided the submarine up through the water, so the top of the submarine was breaking the surface. Water streamed away from the domed window and we were coursing alongside the Debilly bridge. People swarmed the railings, pointing at us and recording us on their phones. I was going to have a lot of viral video proof for my "What I Did This Summer" essay when I got back to school.

"Weird," Nas said. "This is the same bridge where this whole thing started."

He was right. Four days ago, I'd been chasing that kid across the bridge for my backpack and now we'd found a submarine not that far from it. I scanned the faces above us, almost expecting to see the thief, eating my Starbursts.

Instead, in the crowd, I spotted LaForge. She was casually walking away with the goons on either side of her, as if she locked people in an underground dock to die every day. She was carrying her black leather bag with the manuscripts like it was a precious child.

My mom had her hand on my arm and squeezed as I sped up. "Owen, be careful," she said, but I could tell she was enjoying the ride. As we came up closer to LaForge, I brought the sub all the way out of the river.

We bobbed there for a few seconds until LaForge got slowed down by a tour group taking pictures of us. She stopped to see what all the fuss was about, and I connected eyes with her and grinned as she took in Jules Verne's greatest treasure. Her jaw dropped. She may have had a box of manuscripts, but I could tell she was wishing she had the *Nautilus*.

Well, too bad. On my left was a blue button with a trumpet on it, so I pressed it, and a horn blared. Then, a geyser of water shot up from the sub's blowhole. It arched in the air and came down right on LaForge's head.

She crouched down to protect the bag with the manuscripts, but the rest of her was perfectly soaked. She dashed off through the crowd.

CHAPTER FORTY-NINE

We're on TV!

Sunday, June 21, 2:16 p.m.

A FEW HOURS LATER, WE WERE BACK ON DRY LAND, JUST off the bridge. Nas, Rose, and I, plus Bessier and my mom, plus Rose's dad, who was walking on crutches, and Nas's entire family. His cousin Amna had seen viral videos of us stuck on the Eiffel Tower and later landing in the fountain and had shown his family, and they'd immediately come to the scene. Nas's mom was switching between hugging him super tightly and yelling at him for putting himself in danger. "You could have been killed!"

Rose's dad had one arm around her, the other over his crutch, and I heard him saying, "I should never have doubted you." Rose tried to hide a grin as she hugged him back.

I was standing with my mom and Bessier, watching as Officer Sadface talked to them both. "You know, if you'd just answered my questions early on, you could have saved us all this trouble."

He made a sweeping gesture that seemed to cover all of Paris and stopped with the *Nautilus* in the water. "But then again, I suppose you found our missing person." He pointed at Bessier. He sighed. "I might have some questions for you later," he told us. "Don't make it so hard this time. I'm a fan, and I'm on your side."

Mom nudged me. "And you thought you wouldn't make friends here in Paris." With a smirk toward Bessier, she said, "I told you that Owen has a special mind."

"You know each other?" I said.

"A little," Bessier said. "Your mother is a friend of a friend. That's how she came to send your *Great Expectations* paper to me. It was very good."

I blinked. "It was?"

My mom squeezed me. "Of course it was. All that wonderful work about not taking true friendships for granted. I couldn't believe you didn't get a better grade."

338

"Wait...," I started, then shut my mouth. She had read my paper. My original, good paper. The one I'd ripped up because I thought she hadn't cared. "You read that?"

"Yes, many times," Mom said. "That's what I sent to Professor Bessier to get you into the seminar."

He nodded. "And I think that, given the quality of that work—though Dickens is not my favorite—and in light of this, hmm, independent research, you will be getting an A for the test."

I grinned. "Sweet."

"But, you'd better be in class tomorrow and not lose your copy of *Journey to the Center of the Earth*."

Mom shook her head. "He can't make it tomorrow.

He'll need an excused absence, if you don't mind, Professor."

Bessier smiled. "Oh, you have plans?"

"The new *Fast & Furious* is playing," Mom said. "Dubbed in French. It's important Owen immerse himself in the culture."

Bessier tipped his head back and laughed. "I think I can allow that."

Bibliothèque Nationale
de France

Musée des
Arts et
Métiers

Deyrolle

Luxembourg
Gardens

The Catacombs

Epilogue

"GUILLAUME, I'LL FINISH THE DETAILING AT THE BACK OF the *Nautilus*. You can go after you proofread the placards." Sophia Auguste, the new curator of the Musée des Arts et Métiers, took her work very seriously. Chantal LaForge had turned in her sudden resignation, never to be heard from again. Sophia had worked under her for years and was determined to be as good at her job as LaForge had been, if not better.

The new Jules Verne wing of the museum was set to open and would feature the desk he'd worked at from the Bibliothèque Nationale de France, a pair of light-mapping eyeglasses, and a reproduced section of the frieze from Le Dôme on which they showed a map. But the wing's centerpiece, of course, would be the *Nautilus*. The real thing, a high-tech submarine just like in *Twenty Thousand Leagues Under the Sea* that Jules Verne had somehow constructed before his death in 1905. Now every Verne scholar knew where all his money had gone. Sophia Auguste used to dream of the submarine, never imagining it could be real, but now here she was, taking great care to polish every square inch of the marvelous invention.

She was working at the very back of the vessel, in the kitchen—a galley style, with a long dining table just off to the side. Each chair was carved with a nautilus shell and the letter *N*, she assumed for *Nautilus*, or possibly Nemo, and the stove and refrigerator and pots and pans were all a deep emerald green. And now spotless, thanks to her. She cleaned the handles of a cabinet next to a set of coat hooks, prying at them once more. She hadn't succeeded in opening this cabinet yet, and she wouldn't let anyone else try. Guillaume was not delicate; he'd break something. But tonight, it opened. It must have been a pantry, mostly empty now, but there was something at the bottom. Cloth. Camouflage.

She picked it up. It was a backpack. A patch of a

skull was on the outer pocket. It looked far too modern to be here.

Sophia fished around at the bottom of the bag, pulling up a book. She started to laugh. *Twenty Thousand Leagues Under the Sea*, a modern reprint. Inside were underlined pages and notes in a kid's handwriting. She plunged her hand back in the bag, to see if anything else was there.

She came up with dozens of Starburst wrappers.

Then she found a name tag inside. Owen Godfrey.

TO BE CONTINUED...

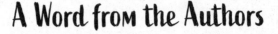

A Word from the Authors

I ALWAYS LOVED GREAT STORIES, ESPECIALLY ADVENTURES and mysteries. When I was a little kid, my father used to read to me every night before I went to sleep. I loved *The Hardy Boys*, but my favorite books were by Jules Verne. In a rocky area on the edge of a field behind my school, I'd hunt for quartz and was positive that I would find a hidden entrance to a tunnel that would take me and my friends Dave and Doug to a prehistoric world in the Earth's core where there would be giant gems, dinosaurs, and glaciers like in Jules Verne's *Journey to the Center of the Earth.* Using a plastic garbage can that we covered in tinfoil and buckets of plaster, my friend Kenny and I made a rocket ship. We used sparklers that we stuck into the plaster and lit. I definitely do not recommend this as a propulsion method for interplanetary travel. Unlike *From the Earth to the Moon* by Jules Verne, we never made it into orbit. The sparklers set the plaster on fire and Kenny wasn't allowed to visit anymore. But more than any other Jules Verne book, I was *obsessed* with *Twenty Thousand Leagues Under the Sea*. I desperately wanted my own *Nautilus* submarine. Using lots and lots of tinfoil (my primary construction material), I covered the walls of a long hallway in our apartment. Every few feet, I made round portholes where I drew pictures of fish and covered them up with plastic wrap so the fish would look like they were behind glass. But the coolest thing I altered was my giant saltwater aquarium. I put tinfoil all around it and made it look like my submarine's windshield. With the aquarium light and water, coral, and the fish, it really looked like we were under the sea.

My *Nautilus* adventure was short-lived, however. We couldn't feed the fish in the aquarium because of the tinfoil, and I had covered up a door that led to a bathroom, so the whole thing had to come down. But I still didn't give up on *Twenty Thousand Leagues Under the Sea*. I got a Super 8 movie camera as a gift and decided to write and film my *own Twenty Thousand Leagues Under the Sea*. Again, using tinfoil, I covered the walls of a walk-in closet and my friend Dave filmed me dressed as Captain Nemo, wearing a snorkel and diving mask and the uniform jacket borrowed from one of the doormen in our apartment building. I just bounced around from wall to wall pretending we were caught in a whirlpool. I don't know how much more of it we filmed beyond that scene and the opening credits. I can't remember the rest of the story, but I do know that it got me interested in telling my own stories. And the more I wrote, the more I read. I love books and also collect them.

One of my favorite things to do is to explore old bookstores, especially when I'm traveling to a new place. We based the bookstore in *The Jules Verne Prophecy* on Shakespeare and Company, one of my favorite bookstores in Paris. You can visit it today. And if you're in Paris, make sure to also check out other real places in the book like Deyrolle, le Musee des Arts et Metiers, and la Bibliothèque Nationale de France. If you skateboard, you should definitely check out Le Dôme. Who knows, you might even find a hidden entrance to a chamber containing a submarine!

—Larry Schwarz

I *loved* to read as a kid. One of the first times I was allowed to visit my hometown library on my own, I had to use the pay phone in the lobby to call my mom for a ride home because there was no way I'd be able to carry and walk home with all *thirty-one* of the books I'd checked out.

Back then my book go-tos were the Baby-Sitters Club, books by Judy Blume and Beverly Cleary, and, later, teen horror novels by R. L. Stine and Christopher Pike. I also loved a series called Choose Your Own Adventure. You've probably seen them: You start the story the same way each time and over the course of reading, make different choices that lead to new plots and outcomes. Maybe it was the budding writer in me that liked the idea of taking charge of the book—did I want to get up close and personal with a giant octopus, or did I want to scuba the heck out of there instead? Why not both?

Those books showed me that writing was inventing. A writer could start with the same basic idea but each would invent a new approach. As I quickly learned by reading the works of Jules Verne to write this book, no writer invented more than he did. He came up with exciting story lines—explorers visit the center of the Earth, or the bottom of the sea, even the moon—but also actual inventions that wouldn't see the light of day until years after his works were published. As we mention in our book, Jules Verne predicted the fax machine, skywriting, and even space travel. In fact, NASA's Apollo XI module, named *Columbia*, took three men to the moon in 1969, more than one hundred years after Verne wrote about a three-man trip to the moon in a ship called *Columbia* in his 1865 book, *From the Earth to the Moon*. Verne even predicted that the launch would take place in the United States and came close to being right on the shuttle's speed! And of course, he predicted electric submarines like the *Nautilus*.

I may not have built my own *Nautilus*, like Larry did, but I hope—like Verne—Larry and I get to keep inventing new stories. What I have learned from Jules Verne is that anything is possible.

—Iva-Marie Palmer

Acknowledgments

WE'RE REALLY PROUD OF THE BOOK YOU'VE JUST READ, but while we get the author credits, *The Jules Verne Prophecy* would not exist without help and support from so many talented and dedicated people.

Thank you to our editor, Christy Ottaviano, for not only seeing the potential of this idea before the writing even began but also for devotedly working with us to make sure the final product lived up to that potential. Thank you also to Fonda Snyder, who gives endless support and encouragement on everything we do. For their work to make *The Jules Verne Prophecy* the best it could be and to get it into as many hands as possible, gratitude also goes to so many others at Little, Brown and Christy Ottaviano Books, including Annie McDonnell, Leyla Erkan, Jessica Anderson, Bernadette Flynn, and Cheryl Lew. Starr Baer deserves a special shout-out for her thoughtful and spot-on copyedits and expert advice, as does Tracy Shaw for designing a thrilling cover, and Michelle Gengaro-Kokmen for putting our words on the page with flourishes and embellishments that make each chapter a treat. Finally, we want to say a huge thank-you goes to Euan Cook, who made characters and settings come to life with his brilliant illustrations (and his willingness to interpret Iva's lousy sketches of runic writing).

Larry would like to specially thank the Band, Alex Cabral, Victoria Cook, Victoria Lewis, Doug MacLennan, Phil Raible, and Michael Valaire.

Iva would like to specially thank her husband, Steve, and sons, Clark and Nathan, for being excellent companions on good writing days and bad. You all make everything worthwhile, and you each have excellent grins. She also owes an abundance of love and gratitude to her parents, Bill and Debra, for constant encouragement of her creativity, for so much love, and for both being avid readers—readers make readers—and to her brother, Bill, for the repeat childhood screenings of *Goonies* and *Raiders of the Lost Ark* on VHS that no doubt helped influence this story. She would list a huge number of wonderful family and friends if not for the fear of forgetting someone and needing several more pages to cover everyone who she's lucky to have in her life.

Finally, we both owe a lot of inspiration to the works of Jules Verne and the enthusiasts and experts past and present who've kept his work alive and relevant for so long. Libraries, librarians, and everyone who strives to keep works of literature available to people young and old are hugely heroic and have our eternal thanks.

Last, to you, the reader—if you've made it this far— books exist to be opened and read. By being a reader, you give stories their power and allow more to be told. Thank YOU.

LARRY SCHWARZ is a creator and producer of live-action and animated series for kids, teens, and families. He's best known for Nickelodeon's anime comedy *Kappa Mikey* and *Speed Racer: The Next Generation*, as well as the live-action series *Thumb Wrestling Federation* for Cartoon Network; *Team Toon*, a Netflix Original; and *Alien Dawn* for Nickelodeon. In addition to *The Jules Verne Prophecy*, he has co-authored *Romeo, Juliet & Jim* with Iva-Marie Palmer. He lives in New York City and East Hampton, New York.

IVA-MARIE PALMER is the author of the middle-grade series Gabby Garcia's Ultimate Playbook, and the young adult novels *The End of the World As We Know It*; *Romeo, Juliet & Jim* (with Larry Schwarz); *The Summers*; and *Gimme Everything You Got*. She lives in Burbank, California, with her husband and two sons.